Dirty Habits
& other stories

Dirty Habits & other stories
BOULEVARD *editions*
London 2005

BOULEVARD *editions*
is an imprint of
THE *Erotic* Print Society
Email: eros@eroticprints.org
Web: www.eroticprints.org

ISBN: 1-904989-08-X

Printed and bound in Spain by Bookprint S.L., Barcelona

The Erotic Print Society is a publisher of fine art, photography and fiction books and limited editions. To find out more please visit us on the web at www.eroticprints.org or call us for a catalogue (UK only) on 0871 7110 134.

JOHN GIBB

Dirty Habits
& other stories

BOULEVARD
editions

EPS

CONTENTS

DIRTY HABITS

Hhigh on the yellowing wall, like a bat with folded wings, Christ hangs from his cross, dead eyes staring down at the stage where a group of nuns sit in a semicircle, their still hands folded in their laps. Before them at the black, wooden lectern stands Sister Berthe. The hall is old with high leaded windows and oak doors and in spite of the chill of the late evening, the windows have been left open. The tang of furniture polish has merged over the years with the institutional miasma of flatulence, sweat and incense common to Catholic boarding schools. Facing the stage on folding chairs are three hundred and fifty teenage boys and a sprinkling of girls, all neat in grey with blue jackets, white shirts and ties. Berthe, tall and angular beneath her cassock, peers over half-glasses clamped on the tip of her nose. She is not smiling. Sister Berthe rarely smiles. On the lectern are loose sheets of paper on which are written the fates of ten of the children sitting before her. The hall is silent. It is Sunday evening, retribution time at Our Lady of Sorrows.

Thirty yards away, in the back row, sits Raymond Gilsenan, a boy of fifteen years from West Sussex who has been in the care of the nuns since he was brought here eight years ago. His Daddy is a Colonel in the Royal Green Jackets. His Mummy is a dead-eyed, piecrust-collared, Army wife. Raymond goes home to Kuala Lumpur in the Summer holidays while at Christmas and Easter, he stays with his Aunty Elsa in the Isle of Man. Across the hall, Wendy Hartwright, sixteen, curly-haired, white-skinned, her skirt short, her jacket a little crumpled, sits fidgeting in her anxiety. The skin of her bottom feels acutely sensitive and she is a trifle breathless; her cheeks pink in spite of the temperature. There is no conversation in the hall. Most of the children are staring at their feet.

As the clock chimes seven in the distant Abbey Church, Sister Berthe taps the lectern with a pencil and looks at her notes, 'In the name of the Father, and of the Son, and of the Holy Ghost,' she says in that Irish lilt, so beguiling to many but redolent of dread to those of us who come within her orbit. 'Every morning when you wake to the sound of the Angelus, you must give thanks to our blessed Lord that your parents have loved you enough to send you here to Our Lady of Sorrows. While you are within these walls, you will be in my care, and as you all know, I take my duty of responsibility both for the redemption of your souls and the success of your schooling, very seriously. Tonight at the end of a day during which we have spent so much time in the worship of our Lord Jesus Christ, we come to the monthly reckoning of the temporal part of the relationship between the community of the Sisters of St. Catherine and those in our care. You will all know to what I refer; tonight is when we discover who has provided a return on the investment in education made by their parents. More important, we will also learn who has not.'

Berthe, pauses and looks around the hall. In spite of herself, she feels a frisson of excitement rippling through her body, a slight increase in the beat of her heart. She adjusts the glasses, picks up the papers from the lectern. 'There are ten of you who, in the opinion of three or more of the community, have failed to demonstrate the required diligence in your academic work. I will read out your names now and you will present yourselves to your head of house immediately after supper.

Two of you, however, Mr Gilsenan and Miss Hartwright, will come to me personally in my room. You two,' she pauses and sighs, looks up directly at the boy in his faraway corner, before traversing the sea of faces to the girl, 'have a history of indolence throughout your time with us and I have decided to make it my personal responsibility to set you firmly back on the path to scholastic endeavour.'

The Headmistress's room can be approached from the boy's Blue Dormitory, through a crumbling archway, down stone steps, along corridors lined with shabby portraits of long dead Abbots, shelves full of unopened leather-bound books and dusty statues of St. Theresa of Lisieux decorated with plastic flowers and cobwebs. When the boy arrives, Hartwright is already there, standing outside the door. Gilsenan glances at her and sees the fear in her eyes. 'Don't worry,' he mutters, 'it will be over quite quickly.' She looks at him, hopeless and alone, on the verge of tears, a lace handkerchief clasped between her fingers. 'I knocked and she told me to wait,' she says. 'I have never been caned before.' As she looks into his eyes, the door opens and Sister Berthe stands, silhouetted in green light from the desk lamp. Gilsenan can see the deputy, Sister Constanza behind her in the room, holding a rod in her hand. He notices that it is black and long and that she is examining it carefully. He is aware of the instrument because it is part of the disciplinary folklore of the school and has been passed down over the years from headmistress to headmistress. He knows that the actress, Brenda de Banzie, was whipped with it when she was educated here in the 1930s. He feels a lump in his throat. 'We'll take you first boy,' says Berthe and, his legs light, his palms slick with sweat, he walks into the room.

Wendy Hartwright stands with her back to the cold wall, her hands clasped behind her. Through the door, she can hear the muffled murmur of the nuns' voices, pick out the words, 'these completely out of the way' followed by 'need to visit the dispensary and see Matron.' Then she hears the sound of the first stroke as it comes clearly through the door. She sees Gilsenan in her mind, kneeling on the chair, stretched over the back, his white flesh, cut and red in the flickering flames from the fire. She winces as the strokes land in measured time, slowly, one after another. After five, she hears him cry, a single, strangled whimper, after eight, she is aware of the gasping of his breath, as if the air is being flogged from his body. Then silence and she knows that her time has arrived and that she will be called to her fate within a few moments. She feels her heart beating as if it is about to burst from her chest and she realises that the most private corner of her body is wet and slick and that she has no idea why.

After a while Raymond emerges from the room, his face red and streaked with tears, he is fumbling with his belt and looking in shame at the floor. As he passes he looks away and without a word, walks slowly down the corridor. 'We'll take you now, child,' the nun looking at her with expressionless eyes, the rod in her hand. As Wendy walks into the room she sees the low prayer stool, two feet high, with a wooden kneeling platform. On the other side of the stool, Sister Constanza, her face flushed, her feet apart beneath her black cassock, her hands on her hips. In the corner of the room, the coal fire glows, black and scarlet, small flames sputtering and crackling in the silence.

Berthe closes the door. 'You're an idle child, Hartwright,'

she says softly, 'and I am going to prove to you that idleness is a sin. What is going to happen to you now is both a deterrent and an incentive. I am sure you will find that this is the first and last time you will be here.' She stations herself beside the prayer stool, the cane held behind her back. 'Now, remove your skirt,' she says, 'kneel down and bend over the top, I will deal with everything else.'

Wendy fumbles with the zip of her kilt, drops the pleated fabric to the floor, bends and picks it up, folds it and places it on a chair. She kneels on the hard wood and leans over the little platform until her hands are on the floor. She is aware of Sister Constanza taking her by the shoulders, pulling her down until her head is gripped between the nun's thighs and she is unable to move. She feels the hands of the headmistress inside the waistband of her cotton pants and the fresh air on her skin as her buttocks are laid bare, she feels her legs being moved apart and she is aware that Constanza has placed a hand on the base of her spine and is pushing down so that her back is arched and her buttocks raised and her sex displayed.

The pain of the first cut reaches her a split second after the sharp sound of the stroke and her body reacts in a reflex movement which brings her head up and into the nun's groin and she can feel the coarse stuff of the cassock and smell the faint scent of cigarette smoke and urine, and the pain comes in waves as the cane rises and falls with all the strength that Berthe can summon from her long body. It feels to the girl that the agony of the world is concentrated in her buttocks and that she is unable to control her physical response. She can hear her shoes clattering on the floor as her feet beat an involuntary tattoo, her face on fire, her eyes streaming.

Finally, it is over and the women stand back and look

down upon the scarlet flesh below them. Constanza adjusts her cassock, a smile on her lips, 'You can run along to the dispensary now Wendy, and see matron,' she says, 'just to makes sure everything is all right.' And the girl breathless with shame and little relief even though it is all over, dresses herself and leaves the study. She wanders through the echoing cloisters and up the bowed steps to the sanatorium and the little room where Sister Benedict dispenses her pills and ministers to the ills of the children in her care. The nun is waiting in her white cassock amidst the reassuring smells of disinfectant, eucalyptus and Radio Malt. 'Turn round Wendy and let's have a look at you,' she says and 'tut-tuts' as she pulls down the girl's white pants, stained now with traces of blood, and washes the wounds and, scooping her fingers into a tub of balm, gently smoothes the cooling cream onto the bruised skin. She takes her time, whispering 'there, there' and slipping her hand between the cheeks of the girls bottom and, almost by accident, down to the wet lips of her vulva and even occasionally into her tight, wrinkled, little anus. 'Now, child, I'm going to keep you here in the San for tonight,' she says, 'after all, you've had a difficult day and I think a little rest away from your friends will give you a chance to reflect on the lessons you have learnt.'

The nun takes the girl by the hand and having made sure that she has washed her face and cleaned her teeth with a nice new brush, ushers her into one of the chambers reserved for sick children. Shafts of moonlight filter through the windows, casting a pale wash on the candlewick counterpanes and Wendy can see that the four dormitory beds with their tubular heads have been pushed together. She undresses in the welcome anonymity of the dark, slips on her pyjama top and climbs between the clean sheets, alone with her thoughts.

Raymond's only desire after his ordeal has been to crawl away and curl into a ball, which he is allowed to do by Matron who suggests that he has a bath and then goes straight to bed. Within ten minutes he is asleep, his knees up to his chin and his thumb firmly in his mouth. His first inkling that he is not alone comes with the movement of air between the sheets and the soft rustling of another body in the room. In his torpor, he stretches his arm, searching for some contact and reassurance until he finds her fingers in the dark. In her vacuum of loneliness, she pulls him to her and drags his arm across her hip and takes his hand and places his fingers on the flesh of her bottom so he can feel the welts on her soft skin, and then their bodies are close together and her hand is against his stomach and her palm on his little cock, as hard and as hot as a poker, and she presses it to her stomach and, after a while, brings up her leg and rolls her thigh over his hip and pulls his head towards her and brushes his neck with her open mouth. It seems to her that they are as close as it is possible to be and as he moves his skinny body instinctively between her legs, she pushes down the palm of her hand and feels him inside the musky, slippery sanctuary between her legs and there is the sudden stab of pain and the faint metallic scent of blood as the flush of heat spreads inside her belly, through her unsullied groin and along the arteries of her thighs and into her stomach.

And as she comes for the first time, crying out in delirium and amazement, she opens her eyes wide and sees across the room, silhouetted in the doorway, the pale shadow of

Sister Benedict, naked, her breasts hanging low, a cigarette smouldering in her red, painted lips.

In her hands she holds a rod.

Escargot Queen

Fontaine bent over the bucket and scooped out a handful of prime Burgundy snails. Starved for a week, they were ready to be cleaned and seasoned; after they'd settled, he would leave them to rest for an hour or two before cooking. There were snails everywhere in Fontaine's kitchen, laid out in their hundreds, shrivelling under layers of sea salt, or boiling in water. Their gritty, slimy excrement would be washed away through ancient lead pipes and sluiced through alluvial grit into the stream behind the restaurant. Standing beside the sweating chef, Rafael, a girl in a green cotton dress, winkled hot cooked snails from their shells and docked their pointed tails with a knife. Her hands were raw and burnt with the work, but she knew better than to show signs of discomfort. When she had removed the boiled flesh, she washed the shells and laid them out in lines on a steel dish where they lay, glistening like regimental buttons.

Fontaine used only the finest *Helix Pomathias*, which he bred in mesh cages, lush with soaking vegetation. He would have them picked from the hedgerows after heavy rain in May or September, and, from the stock, would breed fat, juicy gastropods which he knew would take the powerful flavour of his butter and make it flower in the mouth. He had no feelings for the creatures from which he made his living, other than a vague admiration for their ability to switch from herbivore to carnivore when they needed to. Sometimes, he envied their sexual versatility and would watch them join together, voluptuous with slime and suction, injecting their love darts and copulating for hour after hour.

He chopped eight cloves of garlic, a handful of shallots, parsley, squeezed the juice of a lemon, took a pound of butter and mixed the juice from the boiled snails into the *mélange*. He chewed garlic while he worked, splitting open a clove of the root with his fingers and crunching the tear shaped bulbs as if they were bon-bons, occasionally washing the pungent mouthfuls down with a glass of *eau de vie*.

Gourmets travelled from all over Europe to gorge on Fontaine's *Escargots à la Bourguignonne*. Soft men with rosebud lips and coiffed hair, napkins tucked into their shirts, perched at tables groaning with hundreds of aromatic molluscs, loaves of crusty bread and bottles of fine Mâcon. Sometimes, while the girl Rafael stood tense with muted fear, Fontaine would lift her skirt and place his hot hand between her legs, forcing her to bend across the steel table while he roughly inserted his slippery finger in her tight little anus and, eyes closed and stubby fingers about his cock, ejaculated into the melting butter. He did this, not because he felt any feeling of contempt for his customers, but because he believed that his thick, viscous semen added to the succulence and nutritional power of the dish.

When he was satisfied with the paste, it was chilled and pushed with a palette knife into the empty shells, followed by the cooked escargot which was in turn sealed in with a knob of garlic and butter. When all was ready the regimental squadron of one hundred snails was slammed into the furnace until they began to bubble and the little muscled jewels could be placed into their shallow indentations and served on porcelain plates.

It was late when the last guest paid up and departed, belching into the night. Fontaine sat by the fire and smoked a *Jaune*. His moustache and the stubble on his chin dripped with grease, and the potent scent of the Queen of Alliums oozed through his skin and into the fabric of his worn blue cotton jerkin and striped pantaloons.

By two o'clock it had started to rain and he became aware of the drops clattering on the shutters of the old building, the water streaming down the panes and the condensation misting the edges of the glass. As he looked out, squinting through the downpour, he fancied he saw the face of a girl staring at him from across the courtyard. It was no more than a faint mirage, as if she had crept into the extreme corner of his vision. For a while, he retained a misty picture of greengage cheeks and a garland of soft leaves about a shallow forehead; liquid, half-closed eyes, and a nose like a button above flocculent, amber lips. As he stared and his red eyes began to fill with liquid, the image shredded and left his memory.

When the Michelin clock in the kitchen clicked onto three o'clock, Fontaine drained his glass, banged the cork into the bottle of 'Prune' and threw his Gitane into the embers. He brushed the debris from his apron and, stumbling to his feet, glanced at the girl, crouched in her cot in the corner of the kitchen. The room was spotless now and ready for another day of fecund gluttony. He spat a gob of emerald mucous onto the hearth, untied his apron, slipped on an oilskin and, tripping over the steps into the courtyard, set off along the lane to the village and the cottage he called home.

As he walked, the storm began to blow itself out and the black rain clouds drifted apart to let loose a full moon which cast its white light across the landscape. In front of him the lane stretched away between high hedges and he could see that the old tarmac glittered as if it was covered in diamonds. His feet crunched as he walked, the ground crackling and squishing as his clogs crushed into brittle shells like back teeth cutting through crystallised sugar. He realised that he was walking through a carpet of molluscs and that the weather had somehow brought to life a colony of sodden, wet invertebrates who had made their way cross country carrying their shells on their backs. He sensed from the undulating mass beneath his feet that they were moving down the lane in the same direction as him, and after a while, he found that they were multiplying in number and that he was wading through a rolling sea of soft yellow flesh. His clothes were sodden and heavy with clusters of the creatures which had attached themselves to him and were beginning to weigh him down. They stuck like leaches to his legs and oozed mucus and slime on the fabric of his pants. In spite of his slow progress, Fontaine was unconcerned and paused occasionally to pluck wild garlic from the hedgerow, chewing the roots and spitting the stalks out as he went.

As he drew closer to his home, he could see an aurora of golden light issuing from the cottage as if the old wooden shack was occupied by some ethereal being. He made his way slowly along the muddy path and when he reached forward feeling for the latch, the front door swung back to reveal a dazzling silver room in which the walls and ceiling glistened with trails of mucus, radiating like polished silver glinting in sunlight. The floor undulated with the whorled humps of countless shells and in the centre of the room, suspended above the table and holding an oil lamp, was the girl he had glimpsed from the window of his kitchen.

Now that she was standing before him, he could see that

although she was perfect in every other way, she was no more than a metre in height. Her mouth was small and scrambled like an old rose, her top lip projecting slightly, giving her the appearance of a little girl who has just drunk a glass of milk. Her eyes, wide apart, were slanted above flushed cheeks, and the leaves which formed a crown about her head lay like a pointed cap of pale green from beneath which her hair tumbled in golden curls onto her shoulders.

He touched her tunic which was hard as if cast from green steel and came no lower than her navel, beneath which she was naked. Fontaine, his eyes drawn irresistibly to her sex, began for the first time to feel a tension in his chest, a slight shortness of breath. The child-woman's hairless and dripping pubic mound sat like a hump at the pit of her stomach and he could see the soft lips of her vagina opening and shutting like the mouth of a fish gasping in the well of a boat. On either side of the V at the top of her thighs, a pair of gelatinous antennae waved like seaweed in a current, and the light from the lamp had turned her face to pale onyx. Fontaine turned, unsure, realising suddenly that perhaps he should be elsewhere. As he looked away, the girl leant across and took his cotton jacket in her small fist, facing him and chattering softly until, before he could stop her, she leapt onto his chest, her legs apart, wrapped beneath his arms, her open vagina attaching to his neck and gripping him with irresistible force. Her lips opened as she held him to her and his mouth was in the soft flesh of her stomach. Laughing softly, she threw back her head like a snake preparing to strike, bending her body backwards so that her little breasts flattened on her chest and her golden curls merged into her buttocks and her arched spine. Fontaine, startled and helpless fell back beneath her onto a carpet of hard, splintering shells. He was aware of his own helplessness, knew that she was no longer the child-woman and that she was completely in control of him.

The girl's body was changing from hot and muscular to wet and slippery cold. Her belly and thighs began to glisten and undulate, the crown of leaves hardening and transforming into a whorled carapace of brittle bone, the forehead steepening.

It was as if her body was turning inside out, her face consumed into her flesh and what had been her sex transformed into a wedge-shaped head, antenna lengthening above sightless eyes and a toothless, boneless mouth which was attaching itself to his face. In his sudden blindness and panic, he understood that his clothes, drenched in sputum, were dissolving and being pulled away from his body. He felt a powerful, tumescent muscle attach itself to his chest, binding him together with her, inflicting the most humiliating injuries on his body while coaxing him to a state of sexual delirium. His erection and his inflamed balls were enveloped in wet, pinguid, spongy flesh which palpitated along the muscle of his cock until he could resist it no longer and ejaculated into her, releasing his fluid in a shuddering flood, his roar of ecstasy stifled in his mouth.

For hours, Fontaine lay on his back in the centre of his room, half-absorbed beneath the motionless gastropod while she coaxed tumultuous spasm after spasm from him. He had never experienced such pleasure, made piquant with the infliction of severe pain. And then, after a while, she began to subdue him, slipping bolts of sperm into his bowels and simultaneously flooding him with her soporific fluid, until, when she was content, she began to dismantle him, absorbing his belly and his soft lungs, gorging on the fat of his buttocks and his pungent scrotum. and as he writhed in the throes of ecstasy and death, lingering sumptuously over his garlic infused tongue.

It was all over by the time the winter sun scrambled above the distant hills, casting a solitary rose-coloured beam of light through the window. On the floor, all that remained of Fontaine were a few shredded rags of cloth left in piles around his cock, a solitary little cartilage lying on floorboards slippery with slowly hardening slime. The legions of escargot had returned to their hedgerows, and their Queen, satisfied with her meal and, in fact, quite content with the entire experience, was hibernating in hermaphroditic happiness, safe beneath some corrugated iron in a small paddock behind Fontaine's potting shed.

The Cherry Orchard

Ever since I can remember, we ran around naked, my sisters and I. My mother encouraged it. 'Yes, yes,' she would cry when she found us rolling about the barn covered in spit and straw, 'show God how beautiful you are, you're only children.' Of course, by the time I was nine or so, I had begun to realise that it wasn't really innocent any more. I suppose it was that taint of Catholicism on my father's side which made me ashamed when my skin became so deliciously sensitive. I was experiencing my first glorious sensations of guilt and laying the foundations for what some may call a dissolute life. But, what the hell? My childhood is not just a memory, it has become my guiding light.

One of my earliest recollections is of a holiday in our little farmhouse in the Haute Garonne, a beautiful, crumbling old grange in a fold of hills near Cazères. I remember mother appearing by the pool clutching a slice of lint about the size of an elephant's ear which she carefully attached to my little prick with a piece of Elastoplast to 'save us from that naughty sun'. My consequent erection was such that even the cold water of the pool was incapable of dealing with it and my sister had to rescue me, rubbing away in a business-like manner and saying that it was what nurses had to do every day. It must have been the first rime I came. I suppose I was about nine.

So, ever since I was young, I have been fascinated with being naked in public. The anticipation that a woman, even better, a thousand women, will cast covetous eyes on my beautiful, muscular, uncircumcised cock has become overpowering. The trick has been to arrange the event in a suitably artistic way, which is acceptable to me, and to somehow incorporate the necessary anticipation and heart-stopping fear of discovery. I imagine, in the culture of the *Daily Mail*, I am a 'filthy pervert', which is why I have never talked about it much, except with the likes of you.

When I was eleven, I remember lying innocently naked on the foredeck of my uncle Leighton's speedboat on a hot summer night as we thundered at 30 knots up the east coast of Corfu for dinner at Tulah's. I lay relaxed on my back, my head towards the bows, my young genitals, flecked faintly with salty spray and firm enough to inflame the wind-blown wives gathered in the cockpit. My thighs were fluid in the thrumming air, my cock was on fire. Later, as we moored up on the spindly jetty, I recollect some soft, Irish, middle-aged mouth and a voice telling me to relax and that sweet ejaculation into the warm night.

Adolescence was never really a happy time: those endless monastic months in the Berkshire countryside, cut off from any prospect of satisfactory release. I spent my nights forlornly masturbating over tattered copies of *Spick and Span*, or dreaming of theatrical presentations culminating in the display of my swollen cock to groups of speechless, lubricating matrons. My sole compensation was Fanshawe, a tall, spotty boy and, subsequently, a lifetime adviser, who had perfected a dramatic form of exhibitionism. An expert diver, he would climb to the high board during swimming matches, ensuring that part of his privates were on show to the assembled mothers and fathers. The spectacle of Fanshawe, notionally lost in concentration, preparing for a double pike and twist with a stray testicle protruding from the gusset of his sodden, woollen trunks was for me, a memorable and creatively formative experience.

By the time I was sixteen, I had found a girlfriend and we dutifully messed around during the holidays, but my heart was never in it. I forget her name; she was a sixth former at Down House and she would tell me stories of men loitering in the shrubbery outside the school and occasionally leaping out to expose themselves, much to the amusement of the girls. I never saw any point in this. The attraction to me was the drama, the risk and the meticulous planning behind solitary ventures which were likely to cause a breach of the peace.

Opportunities to indulge myself during my career in the Royal Navy were confined to my return from the Falklands War on *HMS Invincible*. The flotilla, battered and stained with the months of military action, arrived in Portsmouth on 8th August 1982 to a tumultuous reception. I could hear the bands on the quay playing *Sailing* even before we weighed anchor at Spithead. After the days of blood and anger, there was a feeling of anti-climax aboard the old carrier, although not in my case. The ship was dressed overall; 1,500 uniformed ratings, aircrew and officers, all standing to attention along the flight deck as we slipped slowly past the weeping and cheering crowds to our berth in the naval dockyard. A humble helicopter pilot, I alone had the foresight to unzip my uniform and display my trembling manhood to the watching world from a position on deck just aft of the Kojak radar. There is a short piece of film somewhere in the BBC archives where, if you freeze the frame at the correct place and look very closely, you will see a man presenting arms in a manner unbecoming to an officer of Her Majesty's Royal Navy. This is me.

And so I jerked my way onwards into middle age, staging and executing occasional heart-stopping exposures. When I was 31, I became infatuated with the actress Vanessa Redgrave. I adored her assertive, passionate self-confidence, her firm voice and her heavily-nippled, workmanlike breasts, which I had once glimpsed in a badly cut version of the film *Blow Up*. I dreamed feverishly about her genitalia, which I was convinced were generously hirsute and almost certainly Italianate; that is, full of flavour and larger than life. I had to have her. But in my own way.

Of course I had no desire to actually meet the woman because that way lay broken dreams. Her politics repulsed me and, no matter how "eminent" an actress is, one is never safe from exposure to their fanatical self-regard. But I was desperate for her to be aware of me. At the time, she was appearing at the National Theatre in *The Cherry Orchard*, a deeply depressing Russian costume drama which is regurgitated from time to time on the London stage.

My scheme was simple. I commissioned Fanshawe, who fancied himself as a technician in these matters, to build me a nine-inch high, proscenium arch from wire and calico. The device, which was loosely stitched to my trousers, incorporated a pair of velvet curtains, which could be drawn by pulling a cord looped through my belt. He fitted a small battery-powered light, which illuminated automatically when the curtains opened. The device was fixed flat across my abdomen in such a way that I could flick it upright and open the little curtains in a matter of a few seconds. Because Fanshawe had masked the sides with black felt, in the manner of a set of photographic bellows, the display could only be seen from the front. It was a simple matter to position myself so that as soon as the little light switched on, I became clearly visible on the stage.

When the time came, I found myself in the front row of The Olivier flanked by an elderly, emaciated, crop-haired woman wearing a cagoule, hiking boots and a knapsack, and a fat, balding man with a tiny pony-tail and a shabby black suit; both classic examples of today's regular theatre-goer. Fanshawe's advice had been to wait until the curtain calls when the cast tended to look down at the front row, but I disagreed and went for the end of the first act. I knew from my previous visits that this was when Vanessa alone would approach the edge of the stage and look soulfully down into the front stalls.

And so it was. Walking elegantly towards the footlights, she stood still and gracefully lowered her gaze. In the silence, I heard the thunder of my heart, felt it thud against my ribcage leaving me gasping for breath. Immersed in an ecstasy of anticipation, I pulled the cord and, Oh Christ, there was a faint glow in my lap and I could feel the air swirling about my, by now magnificently erect, cock as the little curtains parted. I was so proud. This was the defining moment in my theatrical career.

The sight of my tumescent genitalia framed and professionally illuminated against a black background, had a galvanising effect on the object of my obsession. After a moment of paralysed disbelief, her eyes began to bulge and with a piercing scream she clutched her hands together, raised her eyes to the roof and tumbled unconscious into the orchestra pit. It was time to go.

Unfortunately, while the display was simple to engage, closing the curtains, switching off the light and folding the little theatre flat across my stomach was not so straightforward, particularly while making a break for it along the front row of the orchestra stalls. As I left, I stepped into the straps of the rucksack and, to make it even more awkward, my stumbling arrival at the end of the row coincided with the appearance of two members of the St John's Ambulance Brigade who were carrying their stretcher down the aisle. The rucksack, now open and shedding cheese sandwiches and bottles of water, proved my saviour. 'Don't move,' I shouted at the stretcher-bearers, 'stay still, I believe this is a device.' And I was away through the confusion and out of a side exit.

～

Now I am old, these dramatic events are little more than happy memories. I live alone in Littlehampton and spend my life raising money for disadvantaged boys on behalf of a private charity called the *Fellowship of The Fifteen Felchmeisters*. We have recently raised enough money to pay for our 21st Sunshine coach, a sparkling new Ford Transit, fitted with fifteen seats and a TV. It still makes me very proud. Yesterday morning, I presented the cheque on the steps of the Town Hall in a ceremony attended by all the local media. I always do my best to look smart at these events. On this occasion, I decided on the charcoal grey, three-piece pinstripe, embellished with my gold fob, a pink shirt and stiff, white collar, yellow spotted handkerchief and dark blue silk tie. Just because one is old, one doesn't have to ignore one's standards. It was a jolly little affair and afterwards we all went off to Scott's for a decent lunch.

I'm looking at the press cuttings now. It made the front page of the *Evening Argus*, I'm glad to say, and the photographer did his job well. He's got me in the foreground, holding up one of those four-foot long cardboard cheques and handing it to the smiling Lady Mayoress. "Seventeen-thousand pounds," it reads, "payable to the Royal Variety Club." However, should your eyes stray slightly towards the area of my suit just below the elegant V of my waistcoat, you will notice that I have taken the opportunity to present my compliments to my public, probably for the last time. There it is, clear as a bell if you look carefully; smaller and limper than it once was, but there, nevertheless, for all to see. In Littlehampton.

ONE DAY MY PRINCE WILL COME

Charles stared morosely out of the window, casting his gaze down into the slick, darkening courtyard and its little circle of grass round which the limousines swept in a seemingly endless convoy. He eyed the heavy mustard-coloured curtains with their embroidered ties. It was time someone turned up and pulled them.

Sighing, he looked round to see what was going on in the grate. Logs. Carefully laid out on crumpled copies of *The London Gazette*. Oh God, perhaps someone should come and light the fire?

He shifted in the chair, upholstered in mustard damask by Colefax and Fowler and, parting his knees slightly, stared at the carpet. Heavy Axminster. Cream with a spray of pale pink ostrich feathers in the centre. Hello, it wasn't a carpet. It was a big, fat rug, he could see the edges and the parquet flooring. A bowl of lilies on the piano filled the air with their heavy scent. Oh dear.

He shifted his gaze and examined the portrait of the elderly Edwardian with a centre parting and whiskers. Some golfer from Lancashire called Doctor Stableford. He would have it taken away and put in a cellar somewhere. The clock chimed like a small man hitting a gong. Eight. It would be time for dinner in half an hour. Fish.

A soft knock on the oak door. 'Hello?' he muttered, half hoping that his man would not hear him and go away. But it swung open with a click and there was Cave moving silently into the room and coughing discreetly before placing the silver salver on a table by the Prince's hand. Sherry and a small package wrapped in cloth and tied with ribbon. Charles pushed the packet around the tray with his finger then picked up the sherry and sipped it.

He closed his eyes. He had seen her arrive an hour ago; watched her park the Range Rover and scurry to the portico, doubled up against the rain with her hair in a net and a bulging Barbour clutched tightly around her. He knew instinctively that she had spent the afternoon at Michaeljohn and that she had been getting herself ready for him. He sat up sharply. Perhaps she'd been to that Paki doctor and had another vitamin injection? Oh God.

He cast his mind back to his salad days when the world was full of smiles and he would drive down to Smith's Lawn in the Aston Martin with Pillock sitting in the passenger seat and barking at the policemen on the gate. And there she would be on the veranda outside the Members' Tent, bathed in summer sun and surrounded by admiring men in blazers and tasselled loafers. He knew she would be watching him as he slipped on a clean shirt beneath the oak tree and, light as a feather, mounted his pony.

One blissful Sunday in July she had wandered over, a glittering crystal goblet in her hand, her golden hair a halo against the late afternoon sun. She stood for a moment before handing him a new leather crop with the words "caress me" engraved on a gold band on the stock. His personal protection officer had taken it and put it in the back of the car. It was still around somewhere but had never been certain what to do with it. What was the significance? After all, he had crops of his own. Dozens of them. Nothing had been mentioned since, even when they started making those long mobile phone calls to each other and finally took to going to bed on wet Friday afternoons in the cottage at Bowood.

He picked up the little package and untied the ribbon and there was a leather purse embossed with the triangular crest of the Duchy of Cornwall. He shook the contents onto the table. A single blue, diamond-shaped pill, wrapped in tissue like a sweet, with the word "Pfizer" embossed on one side. Viagra. The tablet lay inert and uncompromising on the walnut veneer while he stared at it as if it was a poisonous insect.

Time stood still for a moment until without warning, the door opened, banging sharply against the rubber stopper before bouncing almost shut. And there with her three-legged walking stick stuck in the gap, was Grandmama, head tilted to one side, hairnet tight across her brow, poised unsteadily on the threshold of the room. Before he could rise from his seat to help her, she moved nimbly towards the grand piano and reached out to steady herself. He knew what had happened, she'd slipped her minders and wandered through the tunnel beneath Marlborough Road. She should have been in bed by now. He dragged his hand down his face and began to struggle to his feet. She had picked up a photograph of herself taken by Barron when she was a young girl down in London for the season. For a while, she stared intently at the picture in its silver art deco frame before turning it over and slamming it down on the polished surface. As he walked forward to take her arm, she turned from the piano and pushed by him.

'Another one of your smutty little floozies, I suppose Charles,' she said and sitting in his chair, picked up his sherry and drained it. He wanted to protest but thought better of it and, anyway, she had the little silver bell in her hand and was ringing it as hard as she could.

'Bring me a bottle of Beefeater and some tonic water,' she

said when Cave appeared, and before sitting back in the chair, reached over to poke her grandson fiercely with the stick. He knew there was nothing for it but to call nurse and have her taken back to Clarence House. Charles opened the door and, as manservant and tray materialised from the gloom, ordered him to arrange for nurse to come and fetch Her Majesty as quickly as possible. But, as usual, Grandmama was having none of it. 'Where's my gin, you idle bugger?' she said as Charles reentered the room and lowered himself nervously onto the velvet foot-stool beside her chair.

'Grandmama,' he said quietly, 'Nurse Galleon is on her way over and you are to go back with her.' But before he finished speaking, she had closed her eyes and was pretending to be asleep.

Within fifteen minutes, nurse had been and gone and the room had returned to its customary torpor. With a sigh, he sank back into the armchair and reached for his replenished glass of sherry. His thoughts returned to the ordeal which lay ahead. He would have his fillet of *Sole Veronique*, watch *The Bill* and retire upstairs at ten fifteen. With any luck it would all be over in an hour and a half and he could drag his aching body away and sleep secure in the knowledge that no one would get past the policeman on the landing. He glanced down at the little table where the remains of the wrapping lay where he had left them.

'Hello,' he said to himself, 'where's the tablet?' He lifted the glass, peered beneath the leather pouch, looked at the floor, knelt down and stared beneath his chair. He rummaged in his pockets but he was wasting his time and he knew it. The Viagra had gone and Grandmama had taken it.

Absent-mindedly pulling at his little finger, he walked to the window and stared, unseeing into the sodden sky, the better to analyse the facts. Arrangements had been made so that at ten thirty he would arrive in the guest suite where he would spend an hour or so in the company of his beloved *maitresse*. Whilst her enthusiasm for the physical manifestation of their mutual affection remained undiminished, the prince's youthful ardour had matured into fondness mixed with respect. To put it bluntly, he knew that, unless he was somehow able to get the old fellow working in a meaningful way, he was doomed. In any second, his man would be here with the fish, but, although no Prince is a hero to his valet, could he trust the man enough to ask for his help? There was nobody else.

In his anguish he heard discreet knuckles brushed gently against the door and then Cave was in the room, head bowed, Chinese lacquer tray in his hands. Within a few seconds, the meal was laid out with the fresh sole, piped potato and white grapes steaming on the plate and the silver and condiments neatly laid out on the occasional table.

As he sat and prepared to eat, Charles coughed, lifted his napkin to his mouth and turned to his man. 'Cave,' he said, 'I have a small personal difficulty for which I need your help.' And out it came, the expectation, the nervous tension, the cooling libido, the waiting, impatient, expectant woman. 'I must go to her, Cave' he finished, closely examining his nails, 'but I have to confess that, at present, romance is far from my mind.' Raymond Cave was one of a long line of domestic servants to the high and mighty for whom discretion had always been a basic part of daily life. He was resourceful and, to an extent, loyal. His secrets were hoarded like jewels and saved in case they were needed in some future emergency. He understood his master's predicament, knew precisely how to deal with it and would not hesitate to do what could to help him. Excusing himself for a moment he retired to his pantry and picked up the 'phone.

In the twilight of her basement room, Galleon dropped the cat gently on the floor and eased herself out of the chair. She stretched the starched cuffs and buttoned the collar of her tunic, pulled the red cape around her neck, straightened the seams of her stockings and inspected the scarlet varnish on her nails. She pulled her hair back in a bunch and secured the crisp white linen cap with a pin.

'Some things never change,' she thought as she walked through the door and pulled it softly to behind her. The lift closed with a sigh as she pressed the button for the third floor. She stared at her feet, at the black patent shoes. Her thighs, encased in shimmering silk were reflected in the perfectly polished toes. She checked her mouth in the mirrored wall and slipped her pointed tongue through her blood red lips. She felt the faint jolt as the door opened and she walked briskly down the corridor, past the guest suite and the painting of *The Long Engagement* by Arthur Hughes, until she came to the uniformed man sitting silent and alert at the little piecrust table. Ignoring him, she knocked gently on the double door and when she heard the muffled, somehow tragic, voice say, 'Come,' she opened it and entered.

He was sitting on the side of the bed, without his trousers, his garters around his calves and his socks tight as paint. He was staring at the floor. Galleon walked across the thickly carpeted room and waited, crossing her arms as she stood by his side.

'Are we sulking?' she asked briskly.

'No, no, no,' he replied, 'just a little tired.'

She paused, turned slightly and stepped in front of him, 'I don't think so, Mister,' she said, 'in fact it looks to me as if Master Bottom Lip has just crash landed in Jutland,' and, raising her voice on the last word, she leant forward towards the bent head, took hold of an ear and twisted it sharply to the right.

It was just like old times. A forced visit to the bathroom, pants down, smack, smack. Jacket, waistcoat, 'Fold please and let's have that shirt off, cufflinks out please. Vest? Into the laundry basket straight away. On with our pyjamas, quickly now before I count to ten.' All done at the double and there he was, in no time at all, hair brushed, in a striped night shirt and ready for bed.

Galleon, suddenly relaxed, lowered herself onto the royal chaise longue and crossed her legs. 'Now, young man,' she whispered softly, 'come over here.' And of course he did, hands by his sides, eyes all but closed, a slight bulge, rising like a plump baguette between his navel and his groin. 'Stand still,' she whispered and, leaning forward while she tilted her head, gently took the royal cock, enrobed now in striped flannelette, between her sharp, white teeth while she breathed hot air through her wet mouth. Her left hand was under the shirt, up between those unresisting thighs, her sharp nails tracing behind the taught skin of his swollen scrotum, her tongue, a little fish, wriggling up and down the underside of his chubby little muscle.

All too soon, he was ready and it was time to go. She stood and took his hand, leading him to the door, his night shirt out in front like the prow of a ship. In the corridor, the chair by the piecrust table was empty, as she had been told it would be. She reached behind her and taking him gently by his now fully-fledged erection, walked him along the corridor to the guest suite where she knocked gently on the door. She left him there, standing alone, a sacrifice to the God of Turmoil.

By the time the door swung open, releasing a cloud of *L'air du Temps* into the night air, Galleon was gone, already standing in the lift as it whispered its way down into the basement.

CHELTENHAM, November meeting; light drizzle, punters hurrying down the avenues en route to the members' restaurant in time for a spot of lunch. This is the world of metal badges, tweeds, grubby Barbours and battered trilbys glittering with autumn rain. Away in the distance, a man with Charterhouse vowels is testing the loudspeaker system while Jockey Club officials take an early tincture in the stewards' room and stable lads in the *Happy Eater* finish their breakfasts and run thick white bread round their plates to wipe up the brown sauce. All is as it should be.

Hubert comes spinning up the hill at 60 miles an hour in his black BMW. On the back seat: a pale green canvas-and-leather case with four pairs of clean jodhpurs, back protector, hard hat, whips, new packet of *Pretty Polly* tights and a pair of hand-made calf-skin riding boots which weigh almost nothing but cost five hundred pounds. Swing into the owners' and trainers' carpark, pull up next to the dark green Bentley Continental, say a respectful hello to the tall man in the full-length camel-hair coat and his plump, blonde wife with her plump red lips and fur hat, 'Morning Guv'nor, morning Ethel', light a Marlboro, clamp it between clenched teeth, swagger down to the gate, turn right to the paddock and through the weighing room into the sacred privacy of the jockey's changing room.

Hubert Delahunty is looking forward to a profitable afternoon; two rides and two favorites. The changing room is packed with the cream of the National Hunt; some naked or in tights, some in neat three-piece suits, three or four sprawled, prawn-pink, in the sauna, some standing around in groups or on mobile phones negotiating the afternoon's spread betting, some sitting quietly and reading *The Racing Post*, some watching the early races at Ayr on TV, one dedicated 30-year-old sitting on the Equiciser. Everyone smoking.

Hubert drops his bag, walks to the table to check his silks and his saddle with the valets and treads his cigarette butt into the cement floor. It is an hour and a half before the first race when he strolls to the physio room, sticks his head around the door and says, 'Hello Bunny'. Bunny is thin as a whip and working hard with her muscular hands on the lower back of Dermot Scully who is lying in great pain on his stomach. 'Flick him in the bollocks with the ultrasound, he's a fuckin' shyster,' says Hubert, slipping out of his Hackett cords and unbuttoning his shirt. He settles in the folding chair at the head of the massage table and lights another Marlboro while Bunny peels magnets off a strip and fixes them like little black parasites over the muscles at the base of Scully's spine.

Hubert, naked, reveals bands of thick tape about his left shoulder and across his thin chest. 'You're a mad cunt, Hubie,' says Bunny as he settles himself carefully face down on the table. 'I'll correct that, you're fucking greedy.' 'Kiss my arse you hard-faced hoor,' says Hubert, while she examines his shoulder and makes him raise his hanging right arm to the horizontal. 'How long has it been?' she says in a resigned voice. 'Uttoxeter, on October 25th.' 'That's nearly a fucking month.' 'Well, I'm fine now. I've been riding out all week.' Bunny takes a handful of oil and starts to work it into the trapezius muscle of the half-mended shoulder. She says, 'Your collar-bone's fucked, Hubert, you need a break. Promise me you'll take it easy.'

Three o'clock and the starter is waiting for some fool to pick himself off the floor and then they are off and Hubert feels the dull ache in his neck until the first fence, but then he is away and the pain and fear are forgotten and there are lumps of mud splattered like shit about his mouth and on his goggles and the five hundredweight of sinew and bone beneath him is hitting through the fences like an armoured vehicle and he can hear the cursing and the thunderous exhalations behind him and the slap of falling bodies in the mud and the howling of the crowd. And then, as if it has been no more than a minute or so, he is coming up the hill at a gallop and is home first by four lengths and looking down at the foaming white sweat on the flanks, and then he is lightly jumping off in the paddock and there, just a couple of feet away, is the plump black hat and the laughing face and the thick red lips.

Five o'clock and the sun has gone now and there is a sullen inevitability about the last race as the horses circle stiffly in the mud half a mile away from the floodlit grandstand, and Hubert's body is rigid with cold and pain and a mist has started to rise about the shredded fences. And then they are off once more and it is only three-and-a-half fucking miles and fifteen runners and what the fuck am I doing here? But, like a half-remembered chapter in a vivid narrative, the scarlet mouth returns to hover like a ghost in the corner of Hubert's eye and they are all over the sixth fence in a thunderous clatter of straining flesh and scything hooves and then they are away into the country for the last time and in front and to the side is Scully with his rain-and-mud-streaked face clamped a few inches over his horse's straining neck and Hubert sees him disappear beneath a tangle of bodies as he hits the thirteenth at 30 miles an hour and goes down with a shuddering crash and then they are away again and there are five of them at the last, jumping it together and his old nag finds something deep within herself down the long finish and brings him home by a neck.

He walks slowly back to the winners' enclosure and jumps off but not so lightly now, and there she is swathed in fur and laughing and looking at him, and he breathes in the comforting warm scents of cigars and wine. 'Walter has had to go, Hubie,' she says. 'He asked me to tell you how happy he is and would you be a darling and drive me home?' And, of course, he smiles and says, 'Yes, of course I will,' as he lifts his saddle carefully onto his throbbing shoulder and walks into the warmth of the jockeys' room and a hot shower.

~

He finds her in a deserted box somewhere high in the grandstand. In the corridors, the Leatherby-and-Christopher girls are cleaning up and there is a clatter of glasses and the whine of vacuum cleaners somewhere in the distance. He shuts the door and turns to her, and she takes his hand and pulls him towards her and into the soft warmth of the black fur, and he puts his arms around her waist beneath the long coat and she is naked as he knew she would be. And he can taste the wine in her mouth and feel her nipples hot and hard through his silk shirt and she has her hand between his legs and his cock is rigid in her fingers, and her coat envelopes them and he has lifted her onto the table and her thighs are around his waist as she pulls him towards her sodden, secret pussy.

But there comes upon him an irresistible longing to bury his mouth into her soaking flesh and he stands back and kneels between her legs and inhales the warm pungency of her loins and feels her strong wiry hair on his lips and her sticky fluid on his muzzle and now his cock is like an iron bar as he stands and enters her and she utters a groan deep in her throat as if she is far away in another world. And he thrusts into her and the waves of heat engulf her thighs and seep into her whole being as he comes and she feels the impact of his ejaculation in the muscular valleys of her swollen, inner self.

'Oops, sorry,' says a girlish voice behind them and Hubert glances at his reflection in the window of the box and sees the flash of a grinning, embarrassed face and a white apron beneath a shock of blonde hair as the door is hastily pulled shut with a click. They dress quickly and smile at each other and leave Cheltenham down the dark wet lanes and along the winding road to Cirencester.

As he drives, she curls up on the seat beside him, the orange lights from the dashboard reflected in her dark eyes, and Paolo Conte groaning on the cassette player. She leans across and he feels her sharp tongue in his ear and she bites him gently on the lobe and takes his hand from the gear stick and puts it on her breast. 'Pull off the road,' she whispers but he ignores her and she leans into his lap and takes his cock and holds his foreskin between her sharp fingers and pulls it back and takes in the head of his resurgent penis between her soft red lips.

~

The Lambourn yard is deserted and in darkness as he hoped it would be and he drives in and parks by a low brick wall. All is quiet; the rain has stopped and the air is fresh with a full moon casting its blue light about the stables, and in the distance the windows of the manor house throw a yellow, elongated glow across the lawns. He takes a racing saddle from the tack room and they walk down the row of boxes until he finds what he wants and slips back the bolt. And in the corner the mare turns and whinnies softly as he slips a halter over her head, secures her to a ringbolt in the wall and throws the saddle across her broad back.

Delahuntey adjusts the narrow racing girth and hangs the stirrups in their place. 'Mount her,' he says softly and crouches down so that she can put her shoe in his hands, and then he lifts her onto the light, tiny saddle and she slips her feet through the stirrups and lies with her breasts above the shoulders of the horse and her back arched over the pommel. Her knees are bent and her legs wide apart and her exquisite rump draped in sable above the saddle. Hubert, naked but for his boots, pulls himself lightly up behind her and moves aside the black fur with a flick of his whip and she is offering herself totally to him in the faint light shining through the window.

With his left hand he entwines his fingers in her black hair and pulls back her head as if presenting her to a fence while he encourages her with a fusillade of sharp cuts from the whip on her sacred, white, moonlit flanks. And she cries out as he rides her, his breath forced in great gasps from his lungs as he lunges into her, his pubic bone grinding in the slippery folds of her pussy while her hand is busy between her legs and her scarlet face is deep in the coarse mane of the patient, mystified mare. And, finally, she feels the surge inside him and turns to look into his eyes as he pulls away and slips his cock between her raw, whipped, buttocks and ejaculates luxuriously onto the dimpled small of her back.

Walter, who has taken his habitual evening stroll down to the yard for a last look at his beloved thoroughbreds, pauses by the tack room door and lights a cigarette. He leans against the wall and listens to the sounds of the night, embellished now with the ecstatic mouth-music issuing from the ruby red lips of his lady wife in a stable just a few feet away. He smokes thoughtfully for a while, carefully grinds the cigarette beneath his heel, turns away and walks back to the house.

LOVE AND DEATH IN THE AFTERNOON

I was orphaned in the late spring of my fourteenth year. My Father never came home from the ruins of Monte Casino and my Mother had fretted and mourned until the chaos was over and she could flee to our old farm deep in the Quercy. I remember that on the tops of the hills were fortified villages with high walls and beneath the walls the vines cascaded in green ribbons into the valleys. On hot summer afternoons there were no sounds but the murmur of insects and the occasional rattle of cars labouring along the valley. At noon on a June day of that year, in shorts and a clean white shirt, I sat on my leather suitcase and waited on the bridge below the battlements of the bastide of Lauzerte. Tractors and horse-drawn carts occasionally went down the road and the dust they raised settled on my shoes and in my throat which was parched with the heat. Beneath the bridge the rocks on the river bed were dry and white from the sun but after a while as I looked down the valley, closing my eyes against the light slanting off the road, I could see a Citroën, materialising when it passed through the shadows of the poplars, occasionally vanishing in the sunlight and dust. After a while, when it came to a halt before me, the dry leaves lying on the roadside fluttered into the air like confetti.

In those days, the men who built French automobiles wasted no time with the conventions of less sophisticated societies. My uncle's Citroën was white and had soft, brown leather upholstery and there were small silver and glass vases fixed to the dashboard. The doors opened at the front so that it was awkward for a woman to leave the passenger seat with dignity because it was her legs rather than her head which first came into view. Being a small boy, I was aware of this but as I got to my feet and the door opened, I saw a young woman with shining black hair and olive green eyes and full red lips who was leaning forward and smiling at me. She wore a floral dress and scarlet high-heeled shoes and she was laughing at some remark which my uncle had made. She said, 'Hello darling, you are my nephew Juan; see I know 'oo you are, come 'ere and give me a kiss', and I went to her and she kissed me on my mouth and I could taste her lipstick and scent the citronelle on her skin. My uncle Pete, wearing a wide-brimmed Spanish hat and smoking a cigarette, sat in the driver's seat. He shook my hand and said, 'Johno, my boy, this is your Aunt Maria of whom I am very fond and who I have recently married in the Catholic seminary at Antibes, and now we are going to take you for a bite of lunch following which we will enjoy a *siesta* before delivering you by automobile to our home in Sevilla. I want you to climb in the back and try not to be sick.' And so I left my home and the little cemetery where my mother lay in the freshly turned earth beneath wilting lavender and roses.

After an hour we arrived in the Moulin du Village at Beauville where we found a *gendarme* drinking a whisky and soda alone at the bar. While my uncle settled into the first of a series of *coupes de pastis* and a discussion about the partisans of Navarre, my new Aunt began my education. She was Portuguese, a dancer from Santa Margarida do Sadao, and she had met my uncle Pete in Madrid where he had taken her to the British

American Club and introduced her to his circle of friends. In those days Ernest Hemingway came regularly to the Club and counted himself as one of the urbane circle of expatriates who drank and played billiards to while away the long, hot nights. It had been reported in *La Libertad* that he had been seen hunting shark and marlin with a Thompson sub-machine gun. 'Emingway, 'e 'ees a fat peeg,' said Maria, 'e kill everything and I 'ate 'eem.' We sat down late in the afternoon and it was the first of many long meals, full of laughter and sunlight while we worked our unhurried way westwards to Bordeaux, and through the Landes to St Jean de Luz and across the border and south to San Sebastian.

My aunt and uncle were more like friends having a good time on holiday than lovers. I could not imagine them in a bed together, although I supposed they must have consummated their relationship. If there was any friction, it was because of the divergence of opinion over Pete's dedication to the Corrida, 'the curse on the Spanish people' according to Maria. But my uncle had been an *aficionado* for as long as he had lived in Spain and he followed the bulls every week because it was part of his life and he revered the bravery and the intoxicating mixture of beauty, fear and death.

After the stews of San Sebastian and Pamplona, we trundled on our way across the arid plains of the Tierra de Campos, taking a diversion to watch Dominguin fight in Avila. It was my first Corrida and the afternoon was full of the discordant sound of the town band and the chanting. '*Los toros de lidia dan y los Toros de lidia quitan*,' which we heard as soon as we arrived in the town. Maria refused to come and walked away in the opposite direction, while my uncle brought me through the crowd into the cool cloisters beneath the arena and out into the blistering light of the ring as the matadors were bowing to the *Presidente* at the climax of the *paseo*. Our seats were close to the *barrera* and beneath us, the fighters, slim and tense, waited, the jewels on their costumes bright in the sun, while the picadors entered on horses which in those days were unprotected. As I sat down, overwhelmed by the ecstasy of the crowd, the first bull, a ton of bone and muscle, came into the ring, confused by the noise and light and enraged as the picadors drove home their lances, the crowd howling, the bull, massive head still raised, charging and inflicting terrible injury on the horses. The picadors in the *tablas* now and the matadors diverting the bull with their capes. And after a while a bugle sounded and the dead horses were dragged away and the second act began with the four peones, dancing and placing their *bandilleras* in the neck muscle of the beast and then leaving the ring as the crowd screamed for Dominguin.

My uncle, unmoved, told me that they were preparing the stage for the kill. A terrible change seemed to have overcome the bull. His natural wildness was gone, the barbed, ribboned harpoons hung loose from the bloody muscle of his neck, his head was down at last and he was moving more slowly. 'He is deadly now,' said my uncle, 'very dangerous and he's still strong, and now you must watch the beauty and bravery of Dominguin and remember what you see.' And I sat, mesmerised as the slight figure of the old matador executed the *pases natural* and the *Veronicas* and the *Paron*, and for the first time I could smell the blood, pain and death as the Matador's body passed over the horns of the bull and the sword slowly penetrated through the muscle and the legs of the animal which folded beneath him.

In late July, we drove south across the dirt tracks of La Mancha, across the Gualdalquivir to Aquilar de Ia Frontera where we stopped for a meal of mariscos, grilled shrimp and beer and a night in the Villa del Duque. My room was white and cool, the long cotton curtains swishing gently as the afternoon breeze whispered through the shutters. The floor, cold to the skin even in the suffocating heat of an Andalucian summer afternoon, was of ancient tiles, the painted patterns faded after years of washing and sweeping. The walls of the room were plain, but for an ivory crucifix above the bed and a porcelain framed mirror. The silver coating of the mirror had begun to flake and fade from old age and you could see only a small part of your face when you glanced into it. Above the bed a fan, fashioned from pale wood and enameled metal, stirred the heavy air. The pillows sighed when I lay back and the oak bed-head was solid and broad and on it was carved the face of Christ, his eyes raised piously to the ceiling.

I had drifted into sleep when she slipped into the room and, although I did not hear her, I must have sensed her presence because I opened my eyes. The translucent curtains floated about her body as she stood by the window and she wore a yellow silk gown and her hair was clipped back from her face with an ebony comb inlaid with mother-of-pearl. She looked at me, and with exaggerated care came to sit on the edge of the bed and I noticed that she wore no lipstick and that her face was flushed and her eyes more than usually bright as if, perhaps, she had a fever. She took my hand and said, 'Your uncle has left to meet his friends in the Hotel Ximinez and says that afterwards he will go to the *corrida* in Jerez.' She slipped her body along the bed and lay next to me. 'Sometimes 'e make me very unhappy,' and she rested her head on my chest so that I could feel my heart beating against the skin of her face. And then her hand was behind my head, her fingers entwined in the hair on the nape of my neck.

Beneath her gown she wore a white cotton bodice, stitched and folded to fit her small bust. She told me once that her mother had said to her, 'always wear a bodice in bed because it will strengthen your breasts and make them firm.' Below her waist she was naked and her belly was flat above the black, oily triangle of hair. Her thighs were muscular and white and her feet were curled as if *en pointe*. She took my hand and placed it on her breast, and when I looked into her eyes which were strained and staring like an animal in a trap, I knew that there was little I could do to stop what was happening to me. And so I clumsily kissed her, and put my hand inside the cotton onto her nipple, and she gave a little cry and opened her mouth and turned her body towards me and moved her leg so that it was resting on my thigh and took my hand and put it between her legs. I had no idea of what drove her or what she expected me to do, but my body was rigid and my mind empty of coherent thought.

When she turned and knelt, her muscled back before me and her breasts and shoulders on the white cotton sheet and her knees separated so that she was spread before me and she took my hand and guided it inside her, I felt the hot, pungent sap of her sex and heard the slick sound of our fingers together as she worked her hand into the folds of her vagina. 'We must not do this,' she said, 'God will punish us,' and she turned and reached for my wrist and pulled me down and close to her until my face was in the black hair between her thighs, while she groaned and dragged me violently across her body so that my cock, now aflame and with a will of its own, was between her buttocks and my hands were on her shoulders and her back was arched like a bow. I can still hear the breath, harsh in her throat and the pungent scent of her as she moved impatiently, reaching back to take me in her hand and guide me inside her, but I have no idea how long it was before I felt the panic which comes from losing control, and all the time, as she moved before me she whispered, 'You must stop, this is not right, you are just a boy.'

But she wouldn't let me go and gripped me in the muscles of her sex while I lost touch with time and place; my body weightless and my senses as sharp as a sword. I felt the blood washing through my groin and in my belly and the rolling, blessed moment of release and in a moment of clarity I saw Maria turn towards me, her green eyes wide, and the scream on her lips, her brown back braced and her body abandoned as she slipped headlong into her little death.

Uncle Pete came back to the Villa del Duque while I was eating breakfast early the next morning. He told me that Marcial Lalanda had killed three strong bulls at Jerez. 'Blood and love, my boy,' he said, 'Blood and love.' There was a smile on his face and a cigar in his hand. 'By the way, is your aunt still in bed? She was angry with me yesterday, I think I had better go up and say hello.'

CAMELOT

As he was in the act of putting his hand on the latch, he heard the Duty Security Officer muttering, 'E's on the way ayout,' into his radio. 'Go away,' he thought furiously, screwing up his eyes in a bate. Even after all these years he liked to think that there were times when the microphones were switched off and the watching eyes were turned elsewhere. He stepped through the door onto a gravelled path which flooded with light at the touch of his foot, forcing him, in despair, to hunch his shoulders, thrust his hands deep into his trouser pockets and hurry across the lawn, down the embankment and into the trees.

There wasn't much peace here either. Roosting pigeons exploded out of the foliage above him and a vixen howled somewhere across the valley. Having no idea who, or what, was responsible for this eerie noise, he started to feel doubly apprehensive. After a while, his eyes became accustomed to the dark and he leant against a tree for a minute or so before pushing himself away and, in a gesture of defiance, piddling noisily into some nettles. While the liquid flowed, he said to himself, hearing the words clearly in his mind, 'This is the first moment I have had to myself for weeks.' As he paused to shake away a stray drop or two, a twig snapped close by and a somnolent South London voice said, 'You all roit sar?'

He zipped up his trousers in fury and walked further into the dark wood following the path illuminated by a faint dusting of starlight, until he came out of the trees and onto a mound above a grassy slope. He sat on the turf and rubbed his hands vigorously up and down his thighs. 'Why me, God?' he asked silently. He cast his mind back nine months to the glorious heat-hazy Tuscan hills and the cool of the morning when he could escape into the Count's estate, while Cherie was cross examining the children after breakfast. The *Carabinieri* were more tactful and discreet than the great Metropolitan clodhoppers who followed him like bloodhounds round the grounds at Chequers. Safe for a short while in this dreamy-sleepy paradise, he could wander through the paddocks and the copses of stunted oaks without the risk of tripping over some crop-haired monosyllabic fat-boy crammed into blue serge chinos, In his imagination he breathed once more the sweetness of the lavender and the scent of the rosebushes planted at the end of the vines. As he relaxed, his memory drifted, irresistibly, to that steaming afternoon when the Count and most of his household had retired to bed after along lunch on the terrace. The table, littered with half-empty carafes and crumbled panini, was abandoned for the solace of a cool bed and the chance of a breeze filtered through shutters at the top of the *palazzo*. 'I've just gotta go and walk off all that food, you know?' he had muttered to no one in particular and had wandered away leaving his family dozing by the pool.

It seemed that the world had gone to sleep. The sun had drained the colour from the landscape, bleaching the red earth and squeezing the energy out of every living thing. Like a mad dog, he walked through the wilting vineyard and up to the summit of the little hill where he liked to think that he could ponder the great matters of state in peace. How far it was from the madness of his colleagues: from Peter's flawed beauty; from the hideous, sexual ravings of the Home Secretary. He was beginning to feel that his heart was not in it any more. It was no longer enough to scan though the social pages of *Tatler* in the hope it would wind him up before a conference speech.

Nowadays Alistair had to read him the Deputy Prime Minister's latest statement on Government initiatives in regional assemblies before he could work up the hatred necessary to convince the masses that it was genuine passion. He lay back on the dry grass and tipped his straw hat over his face. He slept.

It was the sudden loss of sunlight that woke him, a coolness on his brow, a faint rustling. He opened his eyes. She was standing over him, her ankles by his ears and the front of her long, cotton dress draped across his neck. Her underwear, grey silk embellished with yellow ribbon, was tight across her generous bottom. He knew from the legs and the pale lemon stockings that it was the Countess, the wife of his host, the Madonna. He had not heard her approach. Electrified with uncertainty and apprehension, he remained inert, his arms at right angles to his body, like a man on the cross.

Slowly, she bent her knees until her hands reached the hem of the dress, raising it sufficiently to allow her to tuck her fingers into the waistband of her pants and pull them down her long legs. One at a time, she lifted her feet and stepped out of the garment. He could not see her face or, indeed, any part of her upper body; but now he could see her vagina, like a sliced peach, framed on either side with a wisp of fine, curly, black hair, and the line of the pink-brown lips of her vulva and the soft roundness of her unblemished buttocks and the shadowy hint of her little, wrinkled, momentarily hidden, anus.

It was his instinct to say something, to gain control of a

situation in which he was helpless. But where were the words? Phrases flashed through his mind: 'I say to the Lady opposite,' or 'We have inherited a situation which is, quite frankly, not of the Government's making.' His mind emptied and the Countess, having dispensed with her undergarment, now squatted above him and began to urinate over his face.

He had thought about it many times since, but had no idea how long he had lain there. When he staggered to his feet, the sun still shone with its mid-afternoon intensity and there was an oval ring of moist earth which briefly marked where his head had been. He had shut his eyes as the warm stream had engulfed him, flooding into his nose, trickling around his eyes and into his hair and the caverns of his ears. The desire to see in detail what was happening had been almost overpowering, but he had not dared to open his eyes and now, as he looked wildly about him, the landscape was bereft of human life. All that remained were a pair of soft, lemon-yellow drawers, which lay on the ground by his side. He picked them up and slipped them inside his shirt. He could feel his skin drying in the sun. He had never felt so alive. His erection, forced into a downwards projection by the Bushwhacker denim shorts peeked out below his trouser leg like a knuckle.

Hiding the Countess's pants from Cherie had been a triumph of ingenuity: he had managed it by keeping them in one of the red boxes to which only he had the key. Back in London, he had started to wear them during the day, knowing that the no-man's land beneath his suit was probably the one place where they could never be discovered. The only real difficulty had been washing them, but he had taken to sneaking up to the flat during the day when his wife was at work and the maids were finished. He would rinse them in sweet smelling soap and leave them behind a radiator where they would dry in half an hour or so.

There had been some close calls. He had found himself at the Guildhall, standing in the urinals next to Irvine after some dinner, but the Lord Chancellor was, as usual, half pissed and had turned sideways and rested his arm on the wall as he relieved himself. Anyway, being an eminent lawyer, he almost certainly wore women's underwear himself and had probably developed his own evasive techniques over the years.

As the months went by, he had taken to retiring to the lavatory with one of his red boxes for ten minutes or so in the evening. It allowed him to change back to a sensible pair of GAP briefs, which he could happily parade in the intimacy of the private apartment before going to bed. Now, nine months later, the Countess's knickers had become a fundamental part of his precious secret life – a vital link between the gross reality of the daily grind and the mystic event on the Tuscan hillside which made his heart lurch whenever he thought of it.

He sighed and looked up at the cold, starlit sky as the vixen howled again, nearer this time, the mournful cry echoing amongst the hangers and bringing him back to the present. He wished he knew what it was; there was a primitive, feral quality to the noise, which he found alarming. He scrambled to his feet and dusted himself down, slipping his hand inside his trousers to feel the reassuring softness of the silk and the hint of an awakening tumescence. It happened whenever he wore them, the fabric seemed to inflame the sensitivity of his skin. But the entire Cabinet would be arriving in the morning and he had boxes of papers to read. He turned towards the house and set off into the trees.

After the starlit hillside, the wood was black as pitch and

he had trouble finding the path. He had been to Chequers many times but instinctively preferred to stay in the house where there were always people around. Here it was different, the alien trees closed in on him and something was rustling in the undergrowth. He began to hurry. The cry came again, this time close by, a yelping, urgent, primitive scream. Reason told him that it was nothing to worry about, but it was the primeval quality to the sound which unnerved him and he started to run. As he scampered through brambles and young bracken, roosting crows and rooks rose from the trees in clouds, flapping into the air above the dark wood, complaining noisily and alerting the police dogs patrolling the perimeter fence. The action of running served to increase his panic until, after a short while, he burst, wild-eyed, from the trees and onto the wide, manicured lawn a few hundred yards below the house.

At the exact point at which he blundered from the undergrowth, the gardeners had that morning started to erect a small folly in the form of a rotunda incorporating a statue of the Madonna. The "feature", as Cherie called it, was an exact copy of a similar shrine built in the twelfth century by Arturo de la Nobiloni, which now rested in a corner of the Count's Tuscan estate. The stone elements, hand-carved from Dartmoor granite, had been delivered and arranged neatly on the grass and, unable to stop, he fell flat along the length of a pillar, cracking his ankle on the base and striking his temple heavily on the carved stone.

Sensors in the wood had picked up the Prime Minister's progress and as he fell, a group of armed Diplomatic Protection Squad Officers was already making its way across the lawn. The control centre in the house was on full alert and floodlights illuminated the grounds. Dogs barked frantically all round the perimeter and the air was full of the twittering of radio static. A police helicopter was scrambled from behind the house and hovered overhead, its searchlight adding to the garish detail of the scene on the lawn where a doctor crouched over the inert form on the grass. Standing on the terrace, the Prime Minister's wife was anxiously looking down the garden.

He drifted into consciousness, his head full of a throbbing, dull ache. He was being carried fast on a stretcher up the steps and across the terrace towards the back entrance of the house. He moved his hand to grip the waistband of his trousers as, through half-open eyes, he saw his wife walking across the flagstones towards him. The stretcher party trotted wordlessly through the house to the small downstairs bedroom used as the A&E station, where they lifted him gently onto the bed.

Strong, competent hands sat him up and removed his shirt. Someone was taking off his shoes; a doctor was examining his forehead. A voice said, 'We've cordoned off the estate, there's something not quite right here.' He sighed in despair, the thumping of his heart intensifying the pain in his head while he felt a nurse trying to unravel his fingers. 'I can't release his grip,' she said and he heard Cherie, speaking in the no-nonsense voice she reserved for legal argument. 'Don't worry dear,' she said, brushing the nurse aside, 'I'll take care of that,' and he felt her strong hands beginning to prise his fingers away. He closed his eyes. He thought of England.

‘Aren't you hot?’ Boddington looked down from his perch at the top of the ladder and squinted at the boy through half-closed eyes. ‘Course I'm fuckin' 'ot,’ he said. The boy, pale and fair-haired with stick-like legs had been hanging around in the road all morning, bouncing a ball and singing some fatuous football chant in a scratchy, high-pitched voice. Occasionally he would glance up at the sheaves of Norfolk reed that Boddington was weaving onto the old cottage roof and ask, ‘Now what you up to?’ It was irritating but there was nothing to be done except to put up with it. He supposed the boy was lonely, kept back from school after the measles or summat.

He sighed and looked across the sun-dappled rooftops to the shimmering Hampshire Downs. With that perfect clarity unique to early May he could hear the cuckoo, hooting across the river in some distant, echoing wood and, close by, the occasional, throaty call of a moorhen being amorous in the reeds. Thatching was a lonely business which was why he liked it, especially in a luscious English spring such as this. Up here in his solitary world, he could watch and listen; let his mind wander, unleash his imagination.

To protect himself from the heat, Boddington wore a spotted red handkerchief tied round his neck but was otherwise naked to the waist, his back salty after being sluiced with perspiration and dried in the sun. He lay the sheaves and ran the split birch rods in a weave to keep them flat, the fat bushy bunches of reed becoming neat and orderly in his hands. When he looked about him again, he saw that the boy had vanished; gone home for his tea, probably. A girl in a summer dress cycled down the lane, looking up as she passed. He saw the curve of a breast as her dress opened briefly in the slipstream of her progress; her blonde hair in a bob, the short cotton skirt flapping in the breeze behind the bike. He thought of her young legs and her slim bottom, tight in white, adolescent cotton, astride the saddle.

As he worked, he imagined the boy and the girl together in a dusty barn, he saw the evening sun slanting through an ancient, arch-braced doorway, the disintegrating sheaves of hay, the scent of last year's harvest. He could see the girl scrambling through the loose bales, breathless, her dress half-undone, her face scarlet in the afternoon heat. The boy standing in the entrance of the barn, uncertain, his arm entwined round an oak beam. Now they were together, the girl standing close, her nostrils flared like a puppy's, her eyes sparkling. He sees the spittle on her lips, hears the thump of her heart. She curls her arm around the boy, behind his head, her fingers in his short fair hair. She pulls his head down, drags his face into the soft swell of her chest; with her left hand she tears at the buttons of her dress and he sees a flash of her childish breasts, young muscles on her slim body and he imagines her stiff nipples in the mouth of the boy as she moves his head from side to side, crushing his face against her.

She steps out of the dress and reaches hungrily into the boy's pants, her fingers entwining his slim little cock. In a fever of haste, she tears at his clothes until he is naked below the waist and the sunshine is etched in thin bars across his thighs and he is coughing in the dust, and she drags him down onto the straw, her hands linked between his legs and her mouth searching for him and taking him between her perfect teeth and running her little tongue into the funnel of his foreskin until she feels his sweet, fresh penis begin to engorge and swell.

The images half drain from Boddington's mind, leaving him weak in the wash of his imagination. He can see that the lane is deserted and he reaches across the roof for his satchel, pulling it towards him and unbuckling the straps. Inside, wrapped in brown paper is a marrow, a succulent, early-season, green-striped gourd that he had taken from the garden on the way to work. It weighs at least four pounds he reckons, and was aching to be picked. Standing unsupported on the ladder, he takes his knife to dispose of the stalk and cuts a thin slice out of the end of the vegetable, which he sprinkles with fine, cool linseed from a flask in the bag.

Twenty years ago, Boddington met Jasmine Pretty at a Country Music Nite in the village pub. Within six months, he had impregnated her and she had moved into his cottage by the river. Respectable and pretty with receptive buttocks and short, curly hair, Jasmine in her courtship and early marriage had carefully hidden her sharp tongue and filthy temper, but it was not long before Boddington discovered his wife's acute insomnia not to mention hypochondria, her mania for household rules and her resolute conviction that, even in hard times, wives should never sully their hands with earning money.

Jasmine's passion was gardening, and the vegetable plot in front of the cottage had become the talk of the village. The family diet was naturally healthy and fresh with the accent on fibre; the Boddington lavatories were pristine, the wooden seats always down, the end of the pink, soft lavatory paper always hanging by the wall. Boots were to be removed in the porch and kept in the scullery and drinking was frowned upon. The possibility of the occasional cigarette was not even discussed, and as for a joint...

The atmosphere of restraint and regulation which hung in the air like poison gas resulted in the abandonment of conjugal sex at an early stage and the Boddingtons' sterile marriage degenerated into a mutual determination to avoid each other's company as far as possible. The vegetable garden became their only point of contact. Boddington became fascinated by the pumpkins and courgettes, the carrots and onions that rose like rooted rockets from the earth. In the early mornings he would wonder at them as he walked down the path to the little gate.

Occasionally he would pause to fondle their curves, squeeze them gently beneath their shading leaves. Sometimes he would slip his hand beneath the lose earth to feel his wife's potatoes and carrots; firm and full of life. But it was her marrows which entranced him. Which was why, as he looked down at the panorama of the lane and the scattered fields, he was carefully pushing the marrow between some loose bundles of read in the eaves of the cottage. Closing his eyes, he unbuttoned the flap in his leather apron, pulled out his already swelling cock and pushed it slowly into the cool, dripping flesh of the vegetable.

'This is more than some grubby little toss,' he thought as he slowly drove deep into the green fibrous flesh, 'it is my tribute to the God of green things. What is all this juice and all this joy? – A strain of the earth's sweet being in the beginning.' And as he worked away, lost in some fecund exorcism, small bursts of dust rose from the thatch and as the muscles in his neck swelled like chicken breasts, he bent his head and felt the friction of his taut, bunched scrotum sliding over the crackling reeds.

He could see the children in the barn, lost in the delirium of their first passion, blind to their surroundings and gorging themselves on their beauty. He watches them clumsily engage, the girl smiling without humour as the boy does all he can to penetrate her, his hair awry, his back criss-crossed with scratches from the girl and the straw. In his mind he pauses, watching her take her dress and wipe her thighs where the boy has helplessly come. The boy lies on his stomach, his head turned away, the agony of failure etched on his face, and she leans over him, stroking his hair and whispering in his ear until after a while he turns and she takes him in her arms and they lie, mouth to mouth and naked together as the sun turns red and the light catches the swirling motes of dust in the evening air.

Boddington in his dream can hear the comfortable burbling of roosting pigeons, a dog barking at the white skeleton of the moon rising above the fields of young grass. The children, bewitched with each other, still lie, hopelessly entangled, the boy's little cock slowly coming to life, while, her legs stretched wide apart, the girl pulls him roughly down towards her pussy. Boddington sees it with great clarity, so slick and pink and wet, as if anointed with oil. He thinks briefly about the whores he has fucked, about the sucking and the pain, the cunts and the arseholes and the flagellation and the fisting and pissing and the fake passion in the face of which the purity of first love rises like a flower in the desert.

And then he realises that the moment is upon him; the tension in that precious, complicated muscle and the roll, the rise and the acceleration of his unstoppable progress. And, as he comes, his eyes rolling upwards like a dying man, he feels the molten broth of his ejaculation flowing like lava into the soft flesh.

Somebody was shaking the ladder. He looks down, his mind immediately emptying like a draining bidet. On the York-stone path beneath him is a stumpy, red-faced woman in a quilted jacket and Wellington boots. Jasmine. 'What do you think you're doing?' she shouts, oblivious of the possibility that someone may be within earshot. 'Don't answer,' he says fiercely to himself. 'You're shagging my marrows again, aren't you?' It wasn't a question. His head throbs, his eyes ache as if they are full of sand, his prick has wilted and almost disappeared, he leans forward across the reeds in misery and despair. In spite of himself, he feels a sense of shame, like a small boy caught playing with himself beneath the sheets. She shakes the ladder again. 'Come down here immediately and bring the marrow with you. We'll have to sit down and have a serious talk about this.' 'Why do we always have to sit down?' he thinks. 'And why have a serious talk about anything?'

Boddington slowly rearranges himself, reaches beneath his apron and tidies himself up, brushes the dust from his chest, unties his large, red, spotted handkerchief to wipe his face and, reaching down, pulls the marrow gently from its place. He looks wistfully at the dripping orifice and holds it carefully between his hands. 'Goodbye,' he says softly, and turning round, throws it with all his might at the upturned face below.

WINIFRED

Mama was a handsome woman with grey hair and bony shoulders. We were never close but when I was twelve, in a moment of weakness, she allowed me into her bed. It was 1944 and, while Daddy and Uncle Walter were messing about in Egypt, we went to stay at Ballacurrie, my Aunty Baxendale's house in the Isle of Man. Late one night after coming to during a half-waking cauchemar, I had taken my Ever Ready "young soldier's" torch and dragged my teddy and my miserable self out of bed and slipped into her room, and she had reluctantly pulled back the silk counterpane and said, 'All right then Ludo, climb in.' She returned to sleep almost straight away and I snuggled up to a pillow, not daring to move lest she woke. After a while, listening to her rhythmic snoring, I decided to play the cave game and descend into the soft womb of the sheets, wriggling like a fish and flashing my torch with its bulbous lens and tin khaki box of batteries. Mother's nightdress had worked its way above her thighs and I was able to see and scent her for the first time. All of a sudden she became a different being; the austere socialite was transformed into a sparse thicket of hair and a pair of spindly legs. Her thighs were askew and I directed my beam of light into her sex and onto the half open lips and pink, wet, aromatic tissue of her vulva. Best of all, I could see her little brown anus. I remember a small, hairy mole beside the wrinkled flesh, and when I carefully, oh so slowly, moved my face closer to her buttocks for a better look, I scented that fecund, earthy aroma which I have ever since associated with dormant promiscuity. In the morning after I had stickily undressed, I noticed Winifred the housemaid examining my pyjamas and bundling them hurriedly into the laundry basket.

My uncle kept a small bore rifle in the hall cupboard. We were allowed to use it if we saw a rabbit on the lawn or felt like a bit of target practise. I loved the bullets; little grey missiles crimped in brass cartridges and oiled nicely so that the cardboard box they arrived in was slightly stained and smelled like a sewing machine. I fished the gun out after breakfast and shot thirty rounds at a piece of cloth pinned to the oak tree behind the pond. What else was there to do? Behind the house, the racing TT bikes were beginning their practise circuits and clattering down Onchan Hill, decelerating before they arrived at the sharp right hand turn at the bottom. Almost every year someone died, sliding off their Motto Guzzi and hitting the kitchen wall like a human artillery round, leaving their blood and brains smeared on the white-painted pebbledash.

After a while I started to wander round the house, along the oak-panelled galleries then downstairs and through the gloomy kitchen past Winifred bent over the range where she was boiling a pot full of garments, which looked remarkably like my night-clothes. I wandered out through the scullery into the kitchen garden where cousin Evelyn was doing her best to train Rodney the Boxer puppy, which Mother had given her as a birthday gift. There was a small rectangular lawn at the back of the house and between the servants' door and the grass a sunken path bordered by a metal rail extended between the walls. Evelyn, cane in hand, had Rodney standing with his front paws on the railing and was trying to persuade him to dance. I could see that the dog had sustained an erection, a slick, pink, glistening sinew, jutting out above his small leathery balls. As she talked to him, trying to make him jig about, he licked his lips and snuffled and winced as from time to time his mistress flicked him with the rod. The scene had a profound effect on me, left me short of breath and made me feel as if a band had been tightened across my chest. When I was very young, Evelyn had taken me into the kitchen garden and allowed me to watch while she pulled her pants down around her ankles and peed. We had created a game in which we examined each other for medical reasons in hidden parts of the garden. Uncle Walter had discovered us in the fruit cage with our fingers up each other and thrashed us both.

For a while I relaxed on a wicker *chaise longue* in the conservatory, breathing in the fragrance of the roses and the smell of moist earth. Winifred arrived with a long, brass spray and began watering a display of fuchsias arranged in pots on shelves set against the wall of the house. Shafts of sunlight coloured by the stained glass set in the outer walls of the conservatory refracted through the moisture in the air, picking out her starched white apron with squares of red and blue. She seemed oblivious to my presence, stretching and bending so that the curves of her body were accentuated beneath her thin summer uniform. The fine drops of moisture in the air had drenched her cotton blouse revealing a hint of the flesh beneath the fabric and bringing into focus the outline of a breast and a loose curl of wet hair across her cheek. My erection, which had been hanging around like a bad smell all morning, lay on my stomach like a courgette. I was at a loss as to what to do with it.

Mother came in like a ghost, gliding through the door and standing on the pastel, geometric tiles laid out in diamond patterns. I wanted to lie on the floor while she stood above me with her legs apart. She said, 'Ludo, your pyjamas,' and she brought them out from behind her back. They were clean and hot from the drier, folded and ironed. I sniffed them and laid them on my lap. 'Take them to your room, darling,' she said. She was able to say the word 'darling' and make it sound like 'bastard', while I had always thought of 'darling' as a special word, full of love. 'Look after them, won't you?' she added meaningfully and turned silently on her heels before stalking away.

I strolled out into the garden and through the shrubbery at the bottom of the lawn. A soldier was sitting on a log by the potting shed. He was sweating in his khaki fatigues and had a battered Thompson sub-machine gun slung round his shoulders. He was whittling at a piece of stick. A group of Italian prisoners of war were digging potatoes and throwing them lethargically into a small wooden trailer. After a while the guard called for tea and the Italians dropped their tools and gathered round. A small pit had been filled with red clay which was baking and smoking in the midday sun and one of the prisoners began to dig it out, after a while producing a handful of charred skin which he slowly pulled apart in his earthy hands. He beckoned me over; '*Riccio*,' he said, smiling and handing me a sliver of white meat. It was tender and sweet. As I ate it, the squaddie removed the cigarette from his mouth and called out, 'Fuckin' edge'og.'

Lunch was lemonade, tomato sandwiches and pork pies served on a rug on the lawn. Mother and Aunt Baxendale took their food in their rooms but Evelyn stayed with me, kneeling with her skirt rucked up so that occasionally I could glimpse her brown thighs and even her rounded white cotton pants. It was as if everywhere I turned, some new sensation conspired to stimulate my senses. As the day progressed I had gradually become incapable of rational thought and my body seemed to be operating at twice its normal speed. I decided to go to my room and read a book.

A sea breeze was rattling the shutters which had been clipped back against the wall. The race practise was over and the road behind the house was silent and white in the afternoon sun. I lay on the bed and picked up my copy of *The Small House at Allington*, until, after a while I drifted off and it was after four o'clock when I came to with a soft knock at the door. It was Winifred. 'Afternoon, master Ludo,' she said, 'I've come to turn down your bed.' It was strange because I knew the beds were turned after we sat down to dinner, yet this was mid-afternoon. 'Of course, Winnie,' I said, and she came in carrying clean sheets and pillow-cases. I sat on the window seat and watched. She was a tall girl, black-haired with a pale complexion which gave away her Irish blood. I watched as she stripped the bedclothes and leant across the bed from the bottom corner, her thighs apart and her knees slightly bent, while she smoothed the under-blanket before flipping the crisp, clean cotton sheets across the mattress, shaking the goose-down pillows and stuffing them into their new cases. As she leant forward, I could see her calves encased in black and her shoes which were also black and pointed and laced in the front.

As she put the finishing touches to her work, stretching the counterpane and making everything nice and neat, she turned to me and I saw that she was smiling, her cheeks pink and her eyes bright. 'Now, master Ludo,' she said, 'your mother has asked me to talk to you. Why don't we go for a little walk,' and she reached for my hand and gave it a squeeze and I followed her out and up the back stairs.

The servants' quarters were high in the eaves of the house. There was a dusty, mothbally smell as if the rooms were never aired. Before the war, Ballacurrie had been busy with guests and parties and laughter every weekend. Now the servants had gone to fight or to work in the factories and Aunt Baxendale made do with a cook, a housemaid and a gardener. Winifred lived alone. Her room was long and bright with a view down to the distant sea and she lived with an ancient, sagging bed, a bookcase, a wardrobe and a long table with a leather armchair. 'Sit down master Ludo,' she said and eased herself up onto the table so that she was sitting facing me with her feet resting on the chair on either side of my knees.

'You've been looking peaky,' she said, leaning forward and kissing me on the mouth. I stood. I didn't know what else to do. 'Shhh,' she said slipping off the table and coming to me and tucking her hand behind my head. I felt her body hard against me. 'Why so tense, Ludo?' she asked, 'There's no need, look it's very easy, come here,' and she took my belt and pulled it away and unbuttoned my trousers and pulled them down and made me step out of them, and then she was behind me with her strong hands on my poor, swollen little cock and her tongue was in my ear and I could feel her breasts hard on my back, and of course I came immediately, wetly, suspended for the first time in my life in that hot, voluptuous, shuddering trance.

It was only the beginning. She lead me to her bed and I watched as she unbraided her hair, untied the bow on her apron, slipped out of her long skirt and her stockings, put her hands on her hips and stretched her long back. While the sun dipped below the window and turned her skin to gold, she lay beside me and held me until I was calm. She talked about how it was when she came, about the heat spreading like hot oil down her thighs and the drum roll of her heart which sometimes left her unconscious, and she took my hand and put my fingers inside her and then I saw her black hair fanned across my belly as she took me in her soft, red mouth, and after a while she lay, smiling, abandoned, her belly slick with sweat and the molten balm of passion, her arms around my neck, her eyes half closed; and I was breathless and still inside her and even in my helpless rapture beginning to wonder with that debilitating worm of uncertainty, who her lover was, and when, after I returned to my world, she would ever come to me again.

Six Of The Best

I am a dental surgeon. I live in a leafy crescent on the edge of the manicured nirvana of the Wentworth Estate in Virginia Water. Life has been good to me and, whilst I am unmarried, I am not especially lonely although I have always found it difficult to establish a serious relationship with a young lady. I enjoy the phrase 'young lady'. It is the sort of term a headmaster might use to a recalcitrant sixth former whom he is about to discipline. Oh yes, I admit I'm a dyed-in-the-wool disciplinarian, always have been, always will be. I love the crack of palm on flesh, the suffused warmth of pink cheeks, the tear in the corner of the eye, the white cotton knickers, the whiff of debauched pubescence. Just the thought of a pert young schoolgirl across my knee can make my legs turn to jelly and my imagination writhe. My tragedy is that any possible fulfillment has, so far, been confined to my imagination and unsupported by reality.

Wherever I go I keep my eyes and ears open for a hint of female humiliation. I scan the tabloids for 'Spanking Shame of Premiership wife', or 'Public School Head Sacked after Sixth-Former Complains'. I read the magazines, buy *Red Stripe* videos, tape the John Wayne films on TV, but it's no good, I've never been able to capitalise fully on the imaginative residue of my fantasies. One can always pay to experience someone else's humiliation, of course, but the financial implications tend to be so great that it is usually I who finish up being humiliated. And for me there is the added risk of a dream shattered by the air freshener sprayed about to obliterate any trace of the previous *aficionado*.

I once almost succeeded with a young German nurse following a party in Englefield Green. She was the worse for wear after overdosing on Red Bull and Vodka, and circumstances eventually conspired so that I was able to pull down her jeans before putting her across the edge of her bed and spanking her soundly. I am fairly strong, if physically unprepossessing in other ways, and, for some ten minutes, I subjugated her to my will and warmed her impertinent little bottom. It ended in tears of course – mine regrettably – after she attacked me, bludgeoning my precious memories and fracturing my collarbone with a marble bust of Goethe which she kept beneath her bed.

You see, the true spanker is never content with the simple physical act; he wants the inevitable submission, the pretty head downcast in shame and the apology and even the pathetic 'Thank you sir.' It is a delicate and subtle mental picture that we weave, so cruelly and so easily shattered. Perhaps you will understand now why I grab at straws and, when the opportunity arises, do all I can to embalm in my mind evocations of masterful castigation, however elusive or faint.

Then, two months ago, in the course of my researches, I came across a small advertisement in the pages of a magazine. Two simple, yet loin-electrifying words, 'Domestic Discipline', and a telephone number, which I immediately called. Of course it was a recorded message, but a woman, well-spoken, with a clipped, no-nonsense delivery, described clearly what was on offer. 'My name is Miss Helena Frost. I am a severe, Fifties-style governess,' she said. 'I work with Susanne, a young lady in need of correction who, on instructions from me, will lift her skirt and take a firm spanking on her navy-blue school knickers, either over the knee or across the desk.'

I immediately made an appointment, and arranged to visit a quiet, suburban address in Eagle Lane, Whipps Cross, at one o'clock the following afternoon.

My thighs had started to tingle as I listened to the voice of Miss Frost and continued to do so as I looked up the address in the A to Z. There had been a postwar timbre in her delivery of the uncompromising, clipped words. I imagined a despairing mother delivering a pretty teenager to Miss Frost with a plea to 'Do whatever you have to, but set her straight.' Tomorrow would be a heady day.

I drove from Virginia Water in my gold Volvo Estate. I always dress carefully on these occasions, and decided on my brown corduroy yachting cap, a black three-piece Cecil Gee suit and grey patent-leather shoes, a fashionable ensemble which I reserve for discipline and for attending meetings of The British Dental Association.

Whipps Cross is in north London, close by Snaresbrook Crown Court. It is in the nature of these experiences that one arrives a little early, wanders the street, checks out the house, raises one's mood, sets one's imagination alight by visualising the apprehension in the mind of the recipient of one's forthcoming attentions. I strolled past number nine Eagle Lane. It was a semi-detached Edwardian villa, the front lawn a little overgrown perhaps. But parked in the middle was a black Rover Saloon in pristine condition: solid as a lump of granite with fat wheels and soft leather seats. Very reassuring. I walked across the grass to the front door and pressed the bell. I removed my cap and held it before me. My heart was thumping like a pile driver.

Miss Frost opened the heavy oak front door and let me in. Sharp chin, sharp nose, fair hair swept back, 40-something. She was carrying a cane and was dressed in a silk shirt and black calf-length skirt. Over her shoulders, she wore a schoolmistress's cape. I noticed the ill-fitting stockings, which bagged slightly at the ankle, the powdery make-up and scarlet lipstick. 'Come into the schoolroom,' she said and showed me into what had once been a large study at the front of the house.

I folded myself nervously into an armchair and looked around. Two school desks and a blackboard. Standard stuff, but the little touches are what stick in my mind. Bookcases bulging with Angela Brazil, Mrs Fitzherbert and Worrals, schoolgirls' annuals, a school bible; racks of old LPs, gas lights, and thick red velvet curtains. I was in another age.

'Susanne is waiting upstairs. She is an amenable girl. She understands the intricacies of role-play and will accede to your wishes. She is submissive. Normally, I bring her in to be interviewed for a contravention of school rules. I question her, dismiss her excuses and discipline her. She takes a thorough hiding. First I put her across my knee and spank her with and without her navy-blue knickers. Then I use the slipper and follow it up with the strap.' She indicated these implements which were arranged on a small Edwardian velvet-topped table. 'At any stage, I can leave her to you to deal with her on your own. If necessary, it's up to you, she will take a caning. But this costs extra, for reasons I am sure you will understand. Have you any particular requests?'

At this moment, my mind, which, a matter often minutes ago, had been bursting with possibilities, emptied. I simply muttered in what I considered to be a worldly way, 'No, no, I'll leave it in your capable hands. Let's see what develops.'

'Very well,' said Miss Frost. 'Perhaps now would be an ideal time to complete the financial arrangements?' I passed across five crisp twenty-pound notes in a trembling hand. 'I will send Susanne down to see you.' With that, this formidable woman tucked her cane beneath her arm and left.

I was in a fever. The early spring sun was beating on the drawn velvet curtains behind me and the room was swelteringly hot. I could hear the sound of feet on floorboards above my head and after a while the creak of someone walking down the wooden stairs. This would be Susanne; in my mind a girl of seventeen, gently born but defiant, curly red hair, athletic and, most important of all, with a muscular, jutting, rounded, smooth, dimpled bottom set beneath slim hips and encased in crisp, blue, cotton knickers.

There was a soft knock on the door and in the Whipps Cross Schoolroom time stood still. 'Come,' I called in my surgery voice and the door opened and into my presence, head down, hands clasped before her, proceeded a substantial person. She had black hair, a bust bulging like a rockery beneath a white shirt and school tie, navy-blue gym skirt, white socks and flat shoes. It was when she spoke that I began to feel nervous. 'Miss Frost has sent me to see you headmaster,' she said in a strangulated, soprano voice, and curtsied in a less than delicate way. It was difficult to estimate how old she was. Anything from 35 to 55, I thought uncharitably, but I realised that the real problem, now that she was standing before me, was all about sex. I do not mean to imply that I was considering indulging in some hanky-panky with this person. By 'sex', I mean: 'Was she a bloke?' For, once again, my hopes and dreams were lying in shards at my feet. Susanne was around five foot nine, had a long, equine face, and legs which would not have looked out of place in the London Irish second row.

My problem was that I had parted with £100 and I had two

alternatives. First, I could stand up and say, 'I'm off, this is not Susanne, this is a bloke and I want my money back' – a futile hope – or I could sit tight and see how things developed. At this moment, Miss Frost walked back into the room and started to stalk up and down, delivering, as she did so, a stern lecture on the evils of smoking. It appeared that Susanne had been caught with a packet of Du Maurier behind the bike shed and was being asked to explain where she had got hold of them. The questions and responses were professionally executed, I'll give them that; they had done this many times before, I could see, and it was just a matter of time before Susanne was over Miss Frost's knees to receive the first of several vicious attacks on her somewhat stringy buttocks.

In order to carry out this part of the 'fantasy', Miss Frost was sitting on a chair and Susanne was facing away from me. I was hoping to be able to conclude something from a close examination of Susanne's trouser department, but I was to be disappointed for she kept her thighs closely together at all times and all I could see, even when Miss Frost had bent her over the desk and was belabouring her with a razor strop, was a pattern of ambiguous, slightly hirsute, creases.

It was at this moment that Miss Frost paused, wiped her brow and stood back to examine the scarlet criss-cross evidence of her labours. Susanne, or Basil, as I had begun to think of her, was groaning softly as she lay draped across the desk with a pair of rather grubby knickers around her ankles and her legs braced tightly together. 'Now Susanne,' said Miss Frost, a note of asperity creeping into her voice, 'the headmaster is going to complete your punishment, and may the Lord have mercy on your soul.' And with this melodramatic jibe, she walked briskly across the room and handed me the leather belt.

It isn't so much the money, I thought, as I flexed my arm. It's the fact that yet again, my hopes have been dashed, this time by what appears to be a middle-aged man, probably a retired Group Captain, pretending to be a school girl.

The catch was that, in the nature of things, the harder I hit the bastard, the more he was going to enjoy it. 'Look, Miss Frost,' I said, 'very kind of you and all that, but I have to go. I have just remembered a pressing appointment.' And, as I gathered my corduroy hat, stood up and made a move for the door, Susanne managed to unwind herself from the desk and turn round, curtsying once again as I passed by. It was then that I spied it, the tell-tale edge of a strip of Elastoplast taped across the shaved and spotty groin.

So now I knew; Basil, or whatever his name was, was getting his rocks off at my expense and Miss Frost was pocketing the proceeds. Fair enough, I thought as I scampered back to the reassuring security of the Volvo, it's an enterprise culture after all. But, perhaps now you can understand why it's not at all easy being a freelance disciplinarian.

CONFESSION

ather Anthony rises from his stall in the choir, eases his collar and genuflects stiffly towards the high altar. Morning Mass is over and the monks have gone about their business, but the airy vaults of the Abbey Church are still fluttering with echoes of Gregorian chant. The priest glances at the sunlight loitering in the misty archways and sniffs the incense in the dusty air. Comforting sensations; familiar and reassuring; what he is used to.

On Friday mornings, Father Anthony processes the sins of the community in the confessional beside the Chapel of St Agnes. He walks across to the south aisle and, with familiarity born from a lifetime of ceremony, kisses the chasuble, slips it around his neck, settles down on the hard wooden seat and shuts the door. This is the best time of the week; a time to be alone with one's thoughts; anonymous, secure and vulnerable only to muted admissions of human failure. Most of his penitents are regulars, rural Mass-goers who have to scratch around for something worthwhile to get off their chests. Half a dozen Hail Marys for penance and see you again next week. Nothing too challenging.

He sighs and raises a buttock to emit a discreet, low-velocity fart before opening his breviary and turning to St Peter's Epistle to the Apostles. A silence, broken occasionally by the faint chime of a clock somewhere in the distant sacristy falls upon the old building. Father Anthony dozes.

After a while, the door of the Abbey Church swings open and lets in a flood of sunlight. A girl in a flower-patterned dress stands on the threshold. She is black, perhaps of mixed race, and tall; shiny hair swept back from her face and tied in a ponytail. She wears trainers and carries a small leather bag on her back. Her eyes are prominent and limpid, framed beneath a pair of gently slanting eyebrows. Her mouth is generous and her lips are deep. She walks across the nave and into the south aisle. A card slotted into a brass frame on the door announces that Father Anthony will hear confessions between 11.30am and 1pm. She notes the socks and sandals beneath the door, kneels by the grill and says, 'Bless me Father for I have been a very bad girl.'

Father Anthony, who has slipped into a sensuous dream of roast pork, potatoes and crackling, drops his breviary, sits up sharply, crosses himself and mutters, 'God bless you child. How long is it since your last confession?' Deborah, for that is her name, sits back on her heels and says. 'Look, this could take some time, I'm going to get a chair.' As she walks towards the nave, Father Anthony, squinting through the grill, sees her body in a halo of sunshine outlined through the filmy fabric of her skirt.

Settling down, legs crossed, some moments later, Deborah says, 'Look, Anthony, I have no idea how long it is since that catechism shit. I was at school, you know? I need to tell you some of the tricks I been up to lately and get them off my mind, OK?'

The priest, now wide awake, says, 'You must confess your sins my child, but you must realise that I am no more than a vessel; you are speaking though me to Our Lord Jesus Christ and you must truly want to repent. Remember that he laid down his life for our sins.'

'OK,' says Deborah, 'What can I say? I live in Crouch End

with Gig, my boyfriend, and we work in the clubs but not together. He's a barman and he took me in when I arrived here from Los Angeles four years ago. I am still with him and he lets me get on with my life, you know? We may go our separate ways, but we have our own friends and we have things in common, I mean, for instance, we do a lot of drugs.' Deborah takes a tissue from her knapsack and wipes her nose. The priest can think of nothing to say.

'Anyway,' she continues, 'during the summer I meet this man. He is a writer and he comes to the club while he is researching his book. Sometimes he sits in the corner and scribbles on his own, as if he is in another world. This turns me on; I never mix with the customers but writers have a powerful effect upon me so I talk to him a little and we get along. After a couple of weeks, he asks me to have lunch and I say sure, why not? I have never been unfaithful to Gig, but after a while, I realise I am starting to like this guy. His name is Hubert and sometimes he writes stories in the papers and I like his style. He makes me laugh.

'It happens like this. There is a Thai girl working in the club and she is getting married to one of the waiters, so we all give her a big lunch at Quadroon's Bar and Grill in Ladbroke Grove. I am there with Gig but I notice that my beautiful Hubert is also there, standing at the bar, drinking with his photographer friend, Dennis. I catch his eye.

'Well,' Deborah pauses, opens her bag and takes out a small pot of cream with which she anoints her lips. 'To cut a long story short, we nip into the cloakroom to do a line and, oh boy, that's when it happens.' The priest, now very wide awake turns towards the grill and asks, 'What happens?'

'Well,' replies Deborah, 'we are in the disabled and I

turn towards him and kiss him with some vigour. In fact, I smother him with my mouth. I am very oral,' she smiles self-consciously. 'This is a big event for my writer. He stands with his back to the wall and it occurs to me that I have lost control of myself and I have no means of stopping and so I kneel on the floor and I take him in my mouth and I blow him.'

'Blow him?' says Father Anthony.

'Yeah, look, I take his cock out of his pants and I suck it and play with it on my tongue until he comes in my mouth.'

The priest, in what he hopes is a world-weary but reasonable tone says: 'There is no need to be explicit my child. You have confessed to taking drugs and committing a sin of physical impurity and that is all I need to know.'

Deborah uncrosses her legs and leans forward towards the priest's disembodied voice. 'Look, baby, I am not confessing the blow-job,' she says, 'It's not on offer. I have a serious sin here and I need to give it to you.' Father Anthony sits back and reaches once more for his crucifix.

'So, after the event in the toilet, Hubert and I are a fixture,' she continues, 'I call him every day and I see him whenever I can. Sometimes we take a bottle of wine to Airlie Gardens and drink it beneath a chestnut tree and I will sit on his lap, and we do it, slowly and gently until I am weak-kneed and slippery. We go to friends' houses on wet afternoons and fuck each other until we are raw. I love his body and every time I see him or talk to him on the telephone, my pussy gets wet. I cannot get enough of him. One afternoon we go to the Halcyon Hotel and we slide under the bed. There is only eighteen inches between the base of the bed and floor and I lie on top of him in the space. We can hardly breathe because of the pressure and we are covered with sweat and his cock is as hard as an iron bar and hot as a poker and my knees are on either side of his thighs and somehow he slips inside me and I come with a bang; it's so strong because I cannot move my legs or my body.'

The priest, now starting to experience a sensation of claustrophobic unease, says, 'You are telling me a story; there is no need to describe your actions in such detail. It is sufficient simply to say that you have committed an unnatural act.' But Deborah has stood up from her chair and is walking slowly round the aisle of the church. After a few moments, she returns and says, 'I'm talking about love here baby, this is not unnatural, this no sin. I am coming to that. Keep your surplus on, OK?

'Well this goes on throughout the summer and I begin to see that Hubert is becoming more than a little fervent in his regard for me. He gives me flowers and calls me when I am at home with Gig. He drinks more than he used to and he comes to see me late at night when I am counting out the takings at the club. He is interfering with my domestic arrangements. We still fool around from time to time because I find his body so fine, but he is beginning to make me nervous. I think he understands this. Things have changed.'

'Then one night about a month ago, I get a call from his friend, Dennis. He says, "Have you seen Hubert?" And it appears that my writer has disappeared, vanished. None of his friends know where he is and his publishers are looking for him. It is as if he has evaporated. So I talk to a detective I know in the Vice Unit at Charing Cross because I am worried.'

It occurs to Father Anthony that, were he a newspaper man, what he was about to hear would probably make the front page. 'What are you trying to tell me child?' he says. 'Remember that Our Lord has infinite powers of forgiveness.'

Deborah leans forward until the vapour from her mouth condenses upon the metal grill. 'I have found him, Anthony,' she says softly. 'Just now. He's here, in the monastery. I saw him in the garden sitting beneath an apple tree in the orchard. He has a rosary in his hand and is shaved to his skull. He is in the novitiate. My friend the policeman says he has taken the name Paulinus. I thought you should know. He has come here because of me.'

Deborah rises from her chair, pulls her skirt tight about her hips and walks down the aisle and out of the church. After a moment, the priest closes his breviary and stands up. There are no more penitents; the morning sun has vanished behind the clouds and the church suddenly has a sombre feel to it. He raises the chasuble to his lips, folds it carefully on the wooden bench and wanders slowly from the confessional, through the porch and into the garden.

When I Left University, I took it upon myself to follow the family tradition and became a Green. My Mother had, for many years, been Secretary of the Somerset branch of the Campaign for Rural Conservation (CRC), a Council member of the National Trust, a Trustee of the Royal Society for the Protection of Birds and Chairman of the North Devon Ladies Conservative Association. Father had left home when I was at prep school, commenting that his wife had mated with him once twelve years ago and had been trying to kill him ever since.

After I came down, Mummy arranged for me to work at the CRC and now I am responsible for recruitment, which is to say I try to encourage more young people to join. We need to make the government sit up and take notice, but the membership is elderly and unimaginative and my priority is to persuade role models from show business to support us because it is only by associating ourselves with youth and glamour that we will attract young people to the cause.

Last year Pike, the singer and musician, wrote to tell us of his love for the English countryside and how he wants to do what he can for the national heritage. 'Come and talk to me,' he said, 'my heart is overflowing with love for our rural landscape.' This was manna from heaven to my Director, Winifred Peterkin-Cope. 'Run along, Julian,' she said to me. 'Let us get him on board. See if you can winkle a concert out of him. Let's go!'

Pike lives in a sumptuous Regency Villa overlooking

Hampstead Heath. It is set back from the road and the wooden shutters give it the look of a French provincial town house. The front door is painted a glossy sea green and is decorated with an ancient brass knocker in the shape of a Native American head. A Range Rover, a Lotus Elise and a Ford Mustang are parked nose to tail in the drive. My knock is answered by a squat, bloodshot man with a short, lowering forehead, wet lips and thick wiry hair. His cigarette, held low between thumb and forefinger, is angled away from his hip. He tells me that his name is Quince, adding gruffly, as he stands back to let me into the library, that 'Tracey will probably talk to you but Pike is recording in Guadeloupe.' My heart sinks.

So I wait, sitting upright and uncomfortable on a gothic chair in the oak-panelled, book-lined room in the front of the house. There is a Persian rug and a wooden mantle, the surround decorated with Dutch tiles. Someone is moving around upstairs and I can hear Quince as he snuffles angrily in his office beneath the stairs. It is twenty minutes before Tracey appears, waking into the room in a pale green silk dressing gown.

'Lovely,' she remarks, kissing me on the cheek. 'Please excuse me for a few minutes, I have a little duty to perform, then we'll have a drink.' As she speaks, there is a hammering on the front door and a stringy woman appears at the head of a column of twelve primary school children in neat uniforms carrying clip boards. A little Adonis with his grey cap in his hands casts a furious glance at Tracey as she ruffles his golden locks and says, 'This is Hubert, and we all know Hubert, don't we? Now I have a lovely film which I want you all to see.'

'Come on, children,' says the stringy woman, 'sit on the floor. We're in for a treat.'

And then, on the television screen before the silent and curious group, appears Pike in his famous Amnesty concert in Rio. He is giving us his inimitable *Mincing on Venus* and the audience is going wild. And then the scene fades and on the screen appears a bed, and on the bed is Tracey, legs apart and face on fire. And she is giving birth and I am watching, entranced, as the head of a child appears, and then the scene fades and it's back to Rio.

'Now children,' says Tracey, 'I am sure you will all recognize my husband Pike, but do you know what else is happening on the video? No? Well this is Hubert's first venture into the world; a very special moment.'

And so a lesson in childbirth begins and ends, cutting from stage to bed and back until the two themes finally merge and the infant Hubert is delivered and safe in the loving arms of his mother and Pike has reached the climax of his song. I can see that Hubert, mortified, is sitting apart from the class with his head bowed, closely studying the rug and biting his nails.

'Well,' I think to myself, 'that's show business.' After twenty long minutes it is over and the children are in the kitchen drinking goat's milk and eating biscuits.

'The house once belonged to Lord Browning,' Tracey tells me as we stare at some Hockney cartoons hanging next to a series of platinum discs on the staircase. 'Parts of it are Tudor and we bought it in 1996 from David Puttnam. Come and have a look at the bathroom. Pike designed it himself.' And so we stroll around the corridors, looking into bedrooms and staring down from the windows at the Heath, damp and mottled brown below.

As I am trying to pluck up courage to raise the subject of a donation, Tracey hands me her wine glass, saying, 'Hold that a moment, honey,' as she opens a stripped pine door to reveal a fine example of an early Thomas Crapper, decorated in willow pattern motif and with the original wall cistern. 'Keep talking,' she says, lifting her dressing gown and perching on the mahogany seat. I continue to look at her, trying to appear casual as she pees luxuriously, pulling a sheet of paper from the roll and slipping her hand between her legs. Seemingly unaware of the effect she is having on me, she continues her tour of the house. 'You'll like this,' she remarks taking a pole from behind a pair of damask curtains and reaching up to the ceiling to pull down a trapdoor and a hidden ladder, which slides silently down to rest on the floor. 'Won't take a minute,' she says, climbing up towards the brightly lit space behind the hatch. I look up at her long brown legs, which part fleetingly as she stretches to step into the roof.

The loft runs the length of the house and is planted from wall to wall with hundreds of tall green plants reaching hungrily to the light and heat of a dozen ceiling lamps. The air is heavy with moisture from a hidden network of perforated hoses.

'Pike likes to grow his own,' she says, and passes me a small box in which two joints have been neatly wrapped. 'I rolled these myself,' she says, 'Just for you. Let's go down and look at the new bathroom.'

'Erm,' I say, my pulse fluttering like a moth, but she opens another door and we are in a large carpeted room in the middle of which, raised six inches or so on a broad stage above the floor, two baths have been positioned a foot or so apart with a table in between and taps at opposite ends.

Tracey walks across to the window and turns to look at me. A weak sun sinking in the wet sky outlines her legs through the gown, and a mile or so behind her a Jumbo slips past the top of the Post Office tower on its way down to Heathrow.

'We had the taps stolen to order from Blenheim Palace,' she says in a matter-of-fact sort of way. And I walk across the room and stare at the dull silver faucets with their enamel buttons and engraved crests. With a sigh, she turns to reach for a bottle of *Eau D'Orange Vert* and I notice that she has loosened the sash of her gown and let it drop to the ground. As she pours the thick yellow liquid into the bath, the robe separates across her belly and reveals the gentle curve of her pubic bone and a thicket of wiry, black hair. She looks up, arching an eyebrow and staring solemnly at me through the scented, steam-filled room. Well, I suppose I have been waiting for this moment since I first became aware of what a glimpse of thigh could do to me. I have had no real experience of sex, although I was once reduced to a quivering jelly at Ampleforth by a beautiful boy called Ely. So I slip out of my blazer, drop my flannels, tear at the buttons of my shirt and kick off my brogues until I am naked, my heart hammering and my skin tingling as if it had been exposed to something toxic.

Tracey has turned away and is kneeling on the carpet, leaning across the bath to turn off the water. The silk of her gown is stretched tight across her buttocks and she turns to look at me over her shoulder. 'Come round behind me, Julian,' she says and shifts herself slightly so that her knees are further apart and her bottom is raised as if an offering, and I do as she asks and she pulls the green silk aside and waits for me. And so I kneel behind her and put an arm around her hips and hold my cock which has regenerated from a flaccid scrap of gristle into something worthwhile, and slip it slowly up and down her pussy and push myself gently inside her.

But it is not yet to be and, almost immediately and without

a word, she twists away to gather an armful of bath towels from a cupboard and lay them on the floor beside the bath. She takes some green candles from a drawer, lights them and places them around the room, then closes the palms of her hands before her face, bows her head, looks at me and says, 'The act of ritual love-making is a participation in cosmic and divine processes.'

And then she comes to me across the soft carpet, drops her gown to the floor, winds her fingers into my hair and clamps her open mouth to mine, pressing her body hard against my chest and grabbing my balls in her hot hand. Some instinct, reinforced by the fierce grip which Tracey has instituted on my scrotum, forces me to ignore the cardiac fluttering in my chest and do as she wants and to lie on the towel and to open my legs and to look miserably at my prick which is now lying like a blood-sated, tropical leech across the top of my thigh. She sits cross-legged on the floor and faces me.

'This is your *Lingam*,' says Tracey, encircling the old chap carefully with her thumb and forefinger and anointing it with oil from a small silver phial. '*Lingam* is Sanskrit for penis, the wand of light,' and she starts to move her encircling fingers up and down my prick with her left hand while fondling my balls with the right.

Well, inexperienced as I am, I know that it is but a moment before my loins turn to jelly and I ejaculate prolifically into the hot, perfumed, steamy air. But Tracey, understanding well what I am feeling, slows the rhythm of her hand and lightly grips me at the top of my penis so that the imminent eruption subsides. And then she starts again.

'Women are able to climax many times in the *Tantra*,' she says, 'We call it riding the bliss wave.' And so we continue for what feels like hours until my *Lingam* and everything else below my waist is on the verge of volcanic detonation. But, as I reach the moment at which I feel that I can take no more, she turns away from me and leans once more across the bath.

'I am offering you my *Yoni*,' she says, pulling her legs apart to reveal the inside of her glistening, pink, slippery pussy. And she gasps '*Shiva*' as I enter her and she turns her head and looks into my eyes as I slowly and luxuriously flood inside her and float away into oblivion. When I regain consciousness and look at my watch, it is four o'clock and I am covered in a thick towel and lying on my back on the bathroom floor. The water has turned cold and oily in the bath and the candles have guttered down to lumpy gobbets of blackened wax. Hubert has materialized and is standing over me with a cup of tea which is clanking in its saucer. 'Mummy's had to go out,' he says, looking up at the ceiling as if trying to remember his lines. 'She says can you come back again tomorrow?'

LOTUS

Elodie with her green eyes and Titian hair sprawls across a haybail, studying her nails. She thinks that the silver Lotus 7 perched on blocks on the barn floor looks more like a tin can than a car. 'The seats are only two feet wide and the doors are tiny. You'd fall out,' she says. Sebastian's spindly legs protrude like chicken bones from beneath the engine and Elodie's gaze is drawn to the erection lurking in the contours of his crumpled cotton dungarees. He emerges after a minute or so and wipes his hands on a bundle of underpants. 'And where's the bonnet?' asks Elodie, forcing a look of look of pain to flicker across the boy's thin face. 'It doesn't fit actually,' he says, 'I think it belongs to another model.' The chassis and parts were acquired second hand from a post-graduate economics student and Sebastian has unearthed a 1600 Ford Cortina engine in a scrapyard and screwed it to the mountings. 'This isn't very promising,' Elodie thinks.

Elodie and Sebastian are at Cambridge reading Classics and have been together for a month. There's no sex yet, it's 1974, but it was inevitable that she would become Sebastian's girl after her sister Polly abandoned him and flew away to California as a mail-order bride. Theirs is a smouldering rather than a passionate affair. In the evening he meets her at Girton and takes her home. Occasionally their hands touch and sometimes they find that for no apparent reason, they are struck dumb in each other's company.

In February, in a fit of romantic gallantry during a performance of *Tanhauser* at the Operatic Society, he asks her to come with him to Provence after the finals. 'I have friends in St. Tropez, we can drive down in my new car,' he says. And by the middle of May the tubes and aluminium panels have been screwed and riveted together, the engine is in its cavity and the wheels and suspension are bolted in place. It is possible, with a spasm of imagination, to picture Sebastian and Elodie together in the tiny cockpit; the long engine singing before them, as they speed between avenues of poplars towards the distant Corniche.

Four weeks later, released from the terror of finals and wrapped in scarves and leather jackets, they spin down the A11, cross La Manche on the SS. Daughter of Ramsgate, and ease the little car onto French soil on a sunny Boulogne afternoon. Within twenty four hours they have skirted Paris, endured a night of youth hostel separation and arrive in the outskirts of Lyon where they park in *la rue du boeuf* and stroll arm in arm down to the market.

They buy a quiver of crusty baguettes, cold pots of butter, slices of *jambon au foin*, a vine of tomatoes, a *caillette vauclysienne* wrapped in crackly paper and tied with raffia, and cheese and bags of grapes from Mont Ventoux. They spend a few francs on flagons of young, teeth-staining Cotes du Rhone and take a *pastis* in the Café de la Marche before setting off south towards Aix en Provence.

It is lunchtime when they trundle through the sleepy streets of Poujin where Sebastian pulls off the *route nationale* and drives up into the slopes above the valley of the Rhone. They climb through vineyards, fields ribbed with lavender, sweet-scented pine woods and into the clear air of the Ardeche where eagles slip about the hot sky like russet scarves. They find themselves in a landscape of wildflowers and stone walls where occasional cattle with bells are the solitary reminders of human existence. Sebastian spins the wheel and turns between stone pillars into a meadow dotted with cornflowers and abandoned olive trees crouching like old men against the stone walls.

Elodie lays out the food after Sebastian has rolled on the grass to flatten a picnic site. They toast each other from paper cups, cut slabs of terrine and smoky ham with Sebastian's Swiss knife, gorge on sharp cheese and tomatoes dipped in oil and wild basil, anoint their faces with crushed grapes and drink the wine until it is finished and their mouths are stained purple. And when Sebastian stumbles to his feet with a flower of blue chicory to tuck behind her ear, Elodie turns and wraps her fingers in the nape of his neck and for the first time, kisses him on the mouth. It is abrupt and uncompromising and it takes the boy by surprise, squeezing the breath from his body, stifling a cry in his throat. Light headed and holding her to his bony torso, he feels her shoulders beneath the cotton dress, the blood pumping in the veins of her ivory neck, her breasts loose and silky against his ribcage. She presses her belly to him, the sinews of her thighs braced in the pit of his stomach. She tugs his body from side to side; feels the drum of his heartbeat against hers, the heat in his groin, she runs her long fingers down the curve of his spine, pinches the muscles in the small of his back, the soft flesh of his buttocks, his thighs. They lie in crushed, seedy grass, fingers entwined, bodies flaring in the sun, mouths bruised, panting in the Provencale heat.

It is the first time they have seen each other naked or out of control, but the act, when it happens, is little more than a sigh and a moan. Elodie thinks afterwards that, as couplings go, it is at least a beginning and she looks in the white light at Sebastian's half-closed eyes, the straw marks on his flanks, his little cock lying like a drowned canary on his stomach, and she leans down and kisses him and pulls him to his feet, and they dress and climb into the car, Sebastian singing the *Gloria* from *Aida* as they bump their way at speed back to the *Route Nationale*.

Distracted by the emotional release, the Cotes du Rhone and Elodie's hot hand in his groin, Sebastian believes that he is invulnerable. At the cross roads of Pont St. Esprit, momentarily confused by the French habit of driving on the right, he turns north on the left side of the road and after a hundred metres collides with a grey Citroen Pommery *camionnette* with corrugated sides being driven to Monte Carlo by M. Eugene Teil de Champagnat, an antique dealer from Montceau les Mines who is smoking a *jaune* and listening to Edith Piaf on Radio France Sud.

Within a few seconds the little Lotus 7 is no more than a fond memory as the unprotected engine shatters on the chassis and the radiator and front of the old Citroen is crumpled. It is a disaster. M. Teil de Champagnat immediately understands that Sebastian has enjoyed a good lunch and that his car insurance is no longer relevant. He demands cash and the negotiations are completed in the Café des Federations to M. Teil de Champagnat's satisfaction. One hour after Sebastian and Elodie have registered their feelings for one another, they find themselves almost penniless in a dingy bar eighty miles north of the Mediterranean.

As M. Teil de Champagnat prepares to take his leave, tucking Sebastian's holiday money into his old leather purse, Elodie pleads for a lift to St. Tropez, 'We are very young,' she says, 'please don't leave us here.' The transaction has taken place under the cynical gaze of a dozen or so *camionistes* and hard bitten though M. Teil de Champagnat is, he finds it difficult to refuse and so they climb in the back and the old lorry limps slowly away en route to the south.

Inconsolable, Sebastian and Elodie sit on a eighteenth century chaise longue and share a cigarette. A pale light filters through two small windows in the rear doors and they can see that the old Citroen is loaded with monumental nineteenth century French furniture; marble tops, elaborate commodes, tables with fluted mahogany legs and cavernous wardrobes.

While Elodie dozes, Sebastian discovers a dismantled suit of armour wrapped in cloth in a heavy wooden chest. Folded on top is a quilted tunic fashioned from *cuir bouilli*, the boiled hide of a bull. Fascinated, and, it must be admitted, still slightly drunk, he shrugs out of his shorts and begins the long process of arming himself as a medieval knight. He steps into the reticulated steel shoes, fits the greaves and leg guards, buckles on the chain mail gusset. He fits the steel Hauberk round his chest, the shaped shoulder pauldrons and elaborately hinged elbow guards and gauntlets with their spiked gadlings. Fascinated and excited, he drops the mail aventail over his shoulders and lowers the domed and visored bascinet until it rests on his breastbone. Almost unable to move, he leans back against the wall of the van and feels the terrible weight and constriction of the armour on his body, the sweat running down his neck and his already aching spine.

Through the narrow slit in his visor, he sees that Elodie has risen to her feet and is gazing wide-eyed at him. He watches her steadying herself on the furniture as she comes, stepping out of her shorts and dragging the thin cotton shirt up over her head. When she arrives before him, he slowly bends his neck and sees that she is naked and her eyes are half closed, her lips apart.

Elodie is transfixed. She kneels and looks at the figure encased in heavy steel plate. Her mouth dry, she reaches up, slips her hand beneath the leather jerkin to the waistband of the chain-mail gusset. Even through the links of steel, she can feel the heat from his groin and the swell of his erection. She knows he is helpless but she cannot force her hand onto his skin without removing the leg guards and steel shoes. She shuffles behind him, her hands fumbling at the buckles until within 40 minutes, she has exposed Sebastian's legs and feet. She pulls apart the heavy leather tunic and reaches behind to unbuckle the steel gusset.

Released at last, Sebastian's erection springs from his belly like a ferret. 'There's no slack here,' thinks Elodie, 'no room for any more blood.' She takes his cock in her hand and leans forward until it lies between her breasts, bends her head, sucks it up between her lips, holds it tight, feels the power of the engorged muscle, cradles his wrinkled little balls in her hand. The saliva floods from her mouth and the hair in his groin is slick, the veins of his cock blue like rivers on a map.

Sebastian feels that he is about to die. The weight of the bascinet, aventail and Hauberk amount to 80 pounds. Now he wants nothing more than release from the harness into which he has strapped himself, yet the heat of Elodie's mouth and the tension in his groin are irresistible. Elodie turns and pulls a leather armchair towards her until the front of the seat is against his thighs. She kneels with her knees on the curved arms, arches her spine, reaches between her legs to take his cock in her hand, pushes her body back until she has gripped him inside her, pulls her buttocks apart, moves against him. He is helpless, under her control, trapped beneath the weight on his chest.

Elodie writhes and twists, carried away by her desperation. She stands on the chair, clasps her arms behind the steel collar of his helm, brings her legs on either side of his hips and her feet onto the wall of the *camionette* until she is hanging off the front of his body and can guide him inside her again. His spine slopes back, he feels so strong inside her and she lunges, crying and sobbing, feeling him stagger as she comes and comes again. Sebastian, dehydrated, weakened by the heat, his strength ebbing away, finally releases himself into her in a flood as a black veil descends upon him and he falls noisily unconscious to the floor.

While M. Teil de Champagnat continues slowly south, Elodie starts to remove the armour from Sebastian's body. She lifts the visor, pours water into his mouth and touches his lips and Sebastian opens his eyes and groans and it is now that she discovers that they are unable to remove the aventail and bascinet because his face and neck have swollen in the heat and the heavy steel helmet has become stuck.

The clock on the Cathedrale de St. Sauveur is striking six o'clock as the old Citroen pulls into the car park of the Quatre Dauphins. M. Teil de Champagnat dismounts, strolls to the rear of the vehicle. He opens the door and there are the boy and girl asleep in each others arms and naked apart from the old '*casque XVeme siecle et visiere avec une petite cuirasse*' which the boy seems to have slipped onto his head. '*Merde,*' mutters M. Teil de Champagnat and adds, '*les Anglais sont des ecules.*' And so he climbs back into the cab and drives round to M. Rofey at the forge who tut tuts, smiles, eases the neck of the bascinet and removes it.

Even the most implacable of the French Bourgoisie can be touched by the sight of adolescent romance. It is the sudden realisation that the English boy made love to his girl in the ancient *camionnette* while dressed in armour once worn by his ancestor which touches M. Teil de Champagnat. And in a surge of emotional generosity which he will no doubt regret later, he returns their money and says *adieu* on the outskirts of St. Tropez. But he smiles as he lights his *jaune* and puts the Citroen into gear. He turns on the radio. Edith Piaf is singing *Hymne a l'amour*.

Not for the first time, Curzon wakes up in a strange bed. He is acutely aware of himself and of his eyelids as they flutter open. He squints up at the bright light in the centre of the pale blue ceiling but seems unable to move his head. When he swivels his eyes to the right he sees the edge of some white fabric on the periphery of his vision, to the left there is a bowl of geraniums and behind it a thin curtain through which the sun is shining. Why is the light on? He tries to sit up, but, although he is aware of sensations in his body and limbs, he cannot move. He feels no pain, but his head appears to be held in a vice. He tries to speak but no sound emerges. He shuts his eyes and tries to picture what he was doing before he went to bed.

⌒

It is New Year's day and he is sitting on a bench in the jockeys' tent at Barbary Castle, chain smoking and occasionally casting an eye at the girl riders as they change into their silks. At ten to three, he hitches up his tights, steps into his britches and walks through to the scales. After weighing in, he shoulders the saddle and strolls out into the ring. The owner, a tall, pock-marked man with dyed hair, camel-hair coat and velvet sombrero, blows cigar smoke in his face before giving him a leg up onto a decent-looking mare by the name of Scissors. The horse seems lively enough as he jogs her a couple of times round the enclosure. He remembers the girl groom walking by his right foot, her tight black britches, the curve of her back, her face, pink from the east wind, the pony tail swinging in time with her hips.

By three he is at the start, circling with the other riders and waiting for the slow gallop to the first fence in the three-and-a-half mile November Chase. He remembers completing the first circuit, the cursing as the farmers' nags fall away and the distant shouting from hunt supporters standing on their hay bales. He arrives at the thirteenth fence in a bunch, three or four lengths behind the leader. Then blackness. He opens his eyes.

A nurse is leaning over him and with his heightened senses he absorbs her heady scent: her faint floral sweetness endowed with a fleeting residue of skin, saliva, blood and come which makes his heart pound. She says, 'Lord Curzon, I'm afraid you've had an accident.'

～

At the same moment, on the other side of London, McConochie is convinced that he has been banged up. He is on his back in a bare, brightly lit room, unable to move. The police seem to have strapped him to a bed, probably in a cell. The muscles in his arms seem to be tied down at his sides and when he tries to bend his fingers and flex his forearms there is no sensation of touch. It is as if he has been cast in concrete. At his side is a metal frame from which hangs a plastic bag and a tube and he can hear the distant sounds of institutional living, the clatter of plates and the echo of kitchen voices. He casts his mind back to the night before.

～

He is in Islington, in his old Austin Metro, parked in Liverpool Road. Frederick Moodie is in the passenger seat and they are examining the revolver, an ancient Smith and Wesson hammerless .38 with a damaged sight. He has managed to scrounge two rounds of ammunition and they are wearing balaclavas and boiler suits. It is five minutes to midnight. McConochie leaves the car, crosses the road to the Somerfield Supermarket and walks through the front door. He strides to the rear of the building, head down, avoiding the CCTV. The weapon is tucked into his belt. He has left Moodie to stand guard by the line of tills and pushes his way through a pair of plastic doors, up the metal steps and into the office. The manager's room is locked. He pulls out the revolver and puts a round through the keyhole, leans his shoulder to the door and walks in. The manager, a fat man with cropped hair and a beer belly, stands transfixed, two members of staff at his side. Behind them is the open safe. McConochie points the weapon loosely at the group and walks forward gesturing to them to lie on the floor.

It is over in a few seconds. The cash scooped into a bin liner, the phone lines ripped out of the wall, the splintered door jammed shut with a wooden wedge and a shouted warning not to move for ten minutes. The two men run across the road, climb into the car and lock the doors from the inside. A shadow falls across the windscreen as McConochie, his hands slick with sweat, pushes the key into the ignition. Someone between him and the street lamp knocks gently on the glass. He looks up; a man is standing on the pavement, another directly in front of the car and a third by the passenger door. He can see that they are all holding guns. The windscreen implodes.

He opens his eyes, his heart pounding. A police officer is

at the end of the bed and a nurse is leaning over him with her hand on his brow. McConochie says nothing. The policeman, a uniformed sergeant, remarks, 'Jimmy, this is not your lucky day. Shall I tell you where you are? You have become a long-term resident at the Spinal Unit at Stanmore Orthopaedic Hospital. You've been shot in the neck. And do you know who by?' McConochie, silent, turns his gaze upon the man. 'Well, I'll tell you Jimmy. It was the Micks and the amusing thing is that they seem to have had exactly the same idea as you and were not happy when you turned up before them. So, being soldiers of the revolution, they decided to put a bullet in your brain before running away with your hard-earned cash. Unfortunately, as you can see, they cocked that up too and pinged you in the neck. You'll have plenty of time to think about it. Let me know when you're ready to talk. I'll give nurse my card.' He turns away and McConochie can hear him laughing long after he leaves the ward.

It is May and the hospital grounds are littered with daffodils and primroses as McConochie is lowered from the ambulance onto his *Gazelle* battery-powered chair and taken to the Spinal Injuries wing. His fury at what happened to him six months ago has not abated. Moodie, whose injury cleared up in a couple of weeks, has been sent away for ten years but will probably be paroled in four, while McConochie, the criminal mastermind, has been sentenced to a living death. It takes them three hours to transfer him into the hospital Ventilation Unit. 'You'll like it here,' says the orthopedic consultant. 'There's only two of you and you're bound to get on.' He closes his eyes and drifts into a long dreamless sleep.

As McConochie dreams, Curzon stares through the window at the distant city. It is Sunday morning, six months after his fall. Countless hours of orthopedic therapy have given him back the power of speech and the ability to turn his head and shrug his shoulders. The door to the little ward opens and Tulah slips quietly in. His heart lifts as she slides between the bed curtains, pulling them quietly behind her. Her uniform is neat and crisp, the collar white against her neck. She says, 'Hello Sammy, are you ready for your treatment?' He smiles as she reaches beneath her gown and pulls down her pants, before sitting on the bed and opening her legs wide. She looks down, slipping a finger into her pussy, then lifting her green eyes to stare into his. After a while she raises herself onto her knees and turns round so that her bottom is towards him. She lifts her skirt, working herself backwards until she is over his face, and lowers herself gently onto his mouth so that he can taste the salty sweetness of her.

Beneath the sheets she feels his cock begin to swell, a miracle of rebirth in the inert, shattered body. She rummages about amongst the dreadful life-protecting paraphernalia attached to the paralysed torso and finds Curzon's penis now engorged and lying flat across his stomach. As she gently encircles it with her fingers and works at it with long, slow strokes, he comes in a torrent onto her hands and onto the crisp clean hospital sheets. Tulah clears away the sexual detritus and replaces the tubes in their rightful order. 'How do you feel?' she asks after a minute, as she tidies her hair and pulls her tunic straight. Curzon ignores her: 'You'll find some money in my wallet,' he says and closes his eyes. 'I'll call you when I need you again.'

The July sun is beating on the dusty windows of the ward. Curzon is 50 years old today. He lies, wide awake, but with his eyes closed and his mind alert. The only noise is the measured clunk of the ventilation pumps pushing oxygen into the powerless lungs of the two men. At midday, the doors open to admit Lady Curzon in a large hat and pale green Shantung-silk suit, accompanied by her daughters, Kiloran and Mercedes. 'Darling,' she yells, opening her arms and delivering a brace of kisses neither of which are less than twelve inches from her husband's face. 'We've brought you some gulls' eggs, a bottle of Yquem, a pound of Foie Gras from Fortnum's and a packet of those lovely French toasty bits. I'm sure nurse will peel the eggs for you darling. Now how are you?' But before Curzon can respond, a penetrating voice from across the ward provides its own reply: 'I'll tell you how 'e is, you fat old cow, 'e's doing 'is best to catch the fucking clap and I've marked 'im down for a battering.'

The moment's silence following McConochie's verbal ejaculation is broken by Curzon: 'How dare you even address yourself to my fucking wife, you little East-End tosser,' this delivered in a slightly laboured drawl which in turn gives birth to a retaliatory string of expletives, including the phrase 'fat poof so far up your own arse you can't see you've married a woman with a face like a fucking bulldog eating porridge'. Both men, each scarlet in the face, immediately begin to compete with each other as to who can make the most noise. 'Your days are over, you jumped-up chubby chaser. I've got friends, you know, friends who'll turn you into fucking pig food,' is delivered at the same time as, 'My lawyers will have you out of here and in the hospital wing at Belmarsh by tomorrow night.'

A sobbing Lady Curzon and daughters retire to the waiting room and send for the Hospital Security officers who arrive after finishing their 'tea' to calm things down. 'Don't concern yourself m'lady,' says sergeant Paxton gently, 'they tend to get a bit upset with each other from time to time, but they're only letting of steam.'

~

One cold afternoon in November, Tulah arrives in the hospital car park in a black Maserati driven by a large uniformed man of Afro-Caribbean appearance. She adjusts the pearls and smoothes the thin black dress across her hips, walks into the hospital and asks for McConochie. 'I'm his sister,' she says, smiling at the nurse in the office and making her way to the ward. With a cursory glance around the room, she sits on his bed, pulls the curtains behind her and squeezes the lobe of his ear. 'Hello honey,' she says, 'My name's Tulah and Freddie has sent me as a token of his gratitude and respect.' Well, McConochie, flattered and unable to resist, watches as she reaches into her handbag and removes a small battery-driven device known as a *Galloping Major* and a tube of water-based lubricant. Tulah stands beside the bed, pulls back the sheets and fits the device onto McConochie's gradually enlarging penis. 'Now darling, I want you to relax,' she says, and presses the button to GO.

Well, sex for the man with a spinal injury is rarely an apocalyptic event and the most positive benefit is a feeling of relaxation and a lessening of tension. But relief, I'm afraid to say, is not Tulah's objective, because, as the Major works its magic, she leans forward and disconnects McConochie's ventilator from the system. While his complexion turns from pasty white to a darkening blue and his breathing stops, she stands patiently by Curzon's bed. 'There you are Sammy,' she says after a while when the ventilator has been re-engaged. 'All done now. Would you like a turn with my little friend here?' 'You know where the money is,' says Curzon. 'Just take it.' Slowly, with an almost super human effort, he turns his face to the wall.

BLIND LOVE

Spicer strolled through the doorway of the Bristol, down the steps, across the deserted lobby until he stood before the desk. '*M'sieur?*' asked the girl without looking up. 'I have a reservation.' 'Your name?' 'Spicer.' 'How will you pay?' He handed over a credit card, 'I am expecting my wife.' '*Oui, M'sieur.*' The girl passed him a key, '*Dernier étage, M'sieur.*' Looking down, he saw that someone had already relieved him of his case.

He walked across to the lift, a skeletal, *fin de siecle ascenseur* with shiny wooden panels. The liftman, grey haired, formally perched on his wooden seat, stared at the floor. '*Dernier etage,*' said Spicer. The lift rose slowly, the man leaning forward to open the doors as it hissed to a halt. Spicer's room was tucked away down silent corridors and he let himself in, glancing at the lights hanging in a constellation above the bed. His saw that his suitcase had preceded him and been placed on a folding platform by the door and he sighed, smiling to himself, sitting on the bed, feeling the softness of the mattress, lying slowly back, closing his eyes. Sleeping.

~

It was long past midnight when consciousness returned, coming upon him with a shaft of moonlight which sneaked through the curtains and struck soft sparks off the crystals on the chandelier. As his head cleared, he eased his feet onto the carpet, pulled back the curtains and gazed out towards the Madeleine which loomed like a slab of cake above the inky rooftops. He stepped out of his crumpled suit, yawned, rubbed his face, stretched his back. The phone hummed softly, once, twice. He sat on the bed. 'This is it,' he thought. A quiet voice, '*Votre femme est arrivee, M'sieur*'. He slipped on a dressing gown, looked in the bathroom mirror, wondering idly why she was in trouble.

She came into his arms as he opened the door. Florence was smaller than he remembered. He found her mouth, breathed in the Parisian night air from her face, entwined her tongue with his, felt the curve of her bottom through the thin stuff of her dress; fell backwards with her onto the bed, opened his legs, heard her kick away her shoes, felt her fingers in his hair, her breath on his cheek. For a moment he pulled back while she slipped out of her coat. He looked at her face, white in the dim moonlight, saw the tucks at the corners of her mouth, the slant of her eye, the widow's peak. He smelt her; a dark feral scent spiced with citronella; watched her as she pulled her dress above her hips and tucked her fingers into her white pants; felt her breasts fall from the dress as she slipped the buttons. He reached down and moved aside her coat, turned her over so that his cock, inflamed now and hard, lay along the crease of her buttocks.

'No,' she whispered, struggling beneath him until she lay on her back once more, looking into his eyes as she pulled her legs apart, separating, stretching them, holding a foot with each hand, stretching again, knees braced like a ballerina; offering herself. He felt the coarse hair on her pubic mound hard on his stomach, felt the hot, wet flesh as it slipped beneath his cock, heard her cry out as he entered her, felt her shudder as he lanced the chasm of her belly, his groin suddenly wet from her as he slipped his hands beneath her hips, his finger in her pretty, pink, wrinkled anus until he found that he could feel himself through her flesh and then, in the delirium of her orgasm, he joined her, his body curved above her like a figurehead, his eyes above the horizon, staring sightlessly at the silhouette of the Madeleine in the moonlight.

Breakfast arrived at ten o'clock. A discreet knock, followed by a waitress, yellow and black waistcoat tight at her hips, apron to the floor, the trolley crowned with silver trays arranged on a white embroidered cloth, flowers in a crystal flute. She reversed into the room, edging slowly backwards, leaving the food at the end of the bed and departing without turning round, muttering '*M'seiur, Dame*,' as she closed the door. Florence, still half asleep, groaned, turned and brought her knee up gently into Spicer's groin. He saw that she was sucking her thumb like a child, watched her slowly wake, realise where she was, smiling, opening her eyes and leaning forward so that her breasts touched his collar bone. '*Hola*,' she said, running her tongue across her lips, shaking her hair, rotating her shoulders as early morning energy swept through her.

They took breakfast slowly, peeling nectarines with great care, taking champagne from the fridge and mixing it with the freshly squeezed orange juice. They covered themselves with crumbs, Florence making a hole in a warm brioche and slipping it onto Spicer's cock, spreading curls of salty butter and marmalade on her pussy and sighing as he licked her clean while she sucked her coffee from a bowl. He watched as she crawled, naked and warm, down the bed, making her way to the bathroom then pulling out the old bidet with its green, metal wheels and long hose into the bedroom where she started to wash with meticulous care. Spicer watched as she anointed her pussy with oil and trimmed herself with a pair of gold scissors, took a mirror from her bag and examined every inch of her groin and her thighs, pulled herself apart with long fingers, rubbing her pretty little clitoris, pink as a wild berry, as if to lightly lubricate herself for him, while all the time he watched, his heart pounding against his ribs.

And when she was ready, she came to him and led him to the bathroom where she cleaned him as thoroughly as she had cleaned herself. They heard the maid return at midday and take away the detritus of their meal, but they were too busy to break away from the intricacies of their toilet. 'Now there are things that I want you to do for me,' said Florence when, refreshed and tingling, she led him back to the bed and tucked him beneath the sheets. He saw that she had smudged the inside of her thighs with blue powder to accentuate the soft, pastel colours of her vulva and while he watched, his chin sedate on the silk-trimmed blanket, she took a bowl of fruit from the sideboard, lay her pillows beside him and arranged herself on her stomach so that her bottom was raised, her legs apart, knees bent, feet kicking slowly in the air, the bowl by her side.

'*P'tit choufleur*,' she said, 'I have suffered a misfortune which means that I must spend some time away.' And, as Spicer listened with growing interest, Florence told him that the *gendarmierie* were pursuing her and had even issued a warrant for her arrest on suspicion of assault with '*une arme mortelle*'.

'It happened at work,' she said, 'and I am very worried.' Spicer, who had been wallowing in post-coital languor spiked with pre-coital anticipation, returned sharply to non-coital reality, turned his head, cocked an eyebrow and focused on her face.

'Tell me what has happened,' he said. He knew about her job. Amongst other things, it involved unsocial hours at the Alcazar in the rue Mazarine. She never discussed what she did and, for his part, he had not felt inclined to complicate their relationship with activities which occurred outside the bedroom.

But now, she leaned over, bit him softly on the tip of his nose, picked a grape and described how a group of Englishmen had come to the club. They had been there before; middle-aged, coarse men who dealt in the processing of pigs and spent their company's money to entertain buyers from supermarkets in Britain. The Alcazar is small and intimate; a bar, one or two *salles privées*, a room for the cabaret with a dance floor and a dozen or so tables. It is a place where wealthy Parisians go to relax in peace with beautiful women.

According to Florence, *Les Anglais* had, two nights ago, brought with them a man who was staggering, drunk and out of control. He was tall, thin, red-faced, smoked cheap cigars; asked the girls to spend the night with him, pretended to offer them handfuls of money, seemed convinced that he was a man of the world even though he made a habit of public flatulence, which he found amusing. 'You can picture the type of *cochon* this man is?' said Florence. Spicer nodded.

Every morning at one o'clock, Florence and her friend Raphael performed their cabaret. It was the culmination of the night's entertainment at the Alcazar, the prelude to the late hours when the serious business of the night was carried out. It incorporated a Harley Davidson *Electra Glide* doctored by the stage manager to act as a prop, a limited helping of lukewarm lesbianism, a *soupçon* of pussy and a few seconds of mock flagellation with a Brazilian bullwhip. The performance progressed as normal until the *Anglais*, whose name was Postlethwaite, placed his chair on the edge of the dance floor and started inching forward while the act developed. 'By the time I had finished with Raphael, he had moved onto the middle of the floor,' said Florence. 'I began to work the whip. You have to do it slowly, sending the leather cord forward with your wrist, raising it with your arm flexed before moving your hand down, almost in slow motion, so that the tip cracks like a pistol. It's tricky, but I remember watching it snake forward as usual; at the last moment I pulled it back with my wrist. I saw him recoil in the darkness, it comes back to me in slow motion as I think of it, the chair falling backwards, the man's hands clutching at his face. Blood between his fingers, a brief silence before he falls to the floor.'

Entranced, Spicer asked, 'Had he been shot?' 'No, no, no,' said Florence. 'It was the whip. It removed the end of his nose. He was too close, an accident. In the confusion, I ran away. Rafael called to say the flics wanted to see me. I haven't been back since.'

They lay in silence, side by side, Spicer unable to speak. In the outside world a church bell was tolling the angelus and an ambulance was wailing on its way down the Faubourg St Honore. Florence, unburdened, stretched across, wound an arm round his neck, pulled him towards her, took the lobe of his ear in her mouth, ran her tongue into the hollow of his neck, pulled him until he emerged from beneath the warm sheets and lay, his body warm as a freshly toasted croissant, on her curved, receptive back. Sunlight flooded the room illuminating the girl beneath him, catching the motes of dust in the air. He drew back until he was kneeling between her legs, leant forward into the moist cavern of her behind, inhaled her scent, pulled himself along her until he could hear her breathing, feel the flutter of her heart, knew that she was raising herself for him. 'Perhaps you could stay here for a while with me?' he said. 'No one would ever find you.'

It is part of the service at the Bristol that the chandeliers are inspected and cleaned every day. So it was that at one o'clock, M. Roffey together with his aluminium ladder, apron and a wicker basket containing all the necessary cleaning equipment, arrived outside Spicer's room on *le dernier étage*. When his light-knuckled knock was ignored, he slipped a master key in the door, entered the room and erected his ladder at the foot of the bed. Behind him, as he lifted and polished the little cascades of wire and crystal, Spicer and Florence, oblivious to their surroundings, engulfed in their passion, eyes locked together, limbs entwined, breath exploding from their bodies, made love to each other in the Paris sunlight.

They were still at it as Roffey, content with his work, folded his ladder and slipped silently from the room. '*M'sieur, Dame*,' he muttered as he closed the door and ticked off the completed job on his schedule.

'Time for lunch,' he thought.

ARNIE

Arnie stood swaying on the kerb while Westbourne Grove erupted violently round him; red and yellow lights flaring and sputtering like candles plunged in water, the wail of an ambulance, footsteps echoing in the late Bayswater night. His mouth was numb, throat slick with that antiseptic taint, his belief in his invulnerability absolute. When he stepped off the pavement, the car hit him square on the hip and spun him like a top into the twisted metal frame of the bus shelter across the road from The Front Line. Arnie descended into a dreamless sleep from which he never woke.

The girls from The Boulevard were in mourning, but I didn't notice it the following lunchtime as I tucked a napkin into my collar and asked for the menu. By one o'clock Chef was sweating and bellowing orders while waitresses in long aprons bumped the swing doors with their behinds and pirouetted from the kitchen, steaming dishes in their hands. Gopul, his eyes pink with old tears, polished glasses and shook his shaker until the Martinis stood dripping in lines on the bar. Harriet, all in black, busied herself with the bills and spoke to nobody. Someone had pinned a blurred photograph of Arnie by the till, but that was all; he had become a statistic, a tragedy in the West London night.

The driver never came forward and early in the morning when the customers had gone, the girls talked of retribution.

It was the knowledge that someone had killed their friend and got away with it that they hated. One Thursday in March, I picked up the phone on the night desk and it was Harriet.

'Arnie took his pay and wandered off alone after Boulevard had closed,' she said, 'and that was the last anyone saw of him. We all loved him.' I promised to write something for her and scribbled some words for a poster appealing for witnesses. I called my contact in Notting Hill CID.

'Can't help you really, it was a hit and run,' he said, 'probably just a drunk. I'm told your friend Arnie was not exactly in control at the time. Of course, it could have been deliberate, who knows? We're still looking at the forensics.'

But nothing came of it. The flowers laid beside the bus shelter wilted and died and the traffic police filed their reports away. Then I asked Harriet to meet me for lunch at The Bluebird.

'You know I have a boyfriend,' she said.

'Of course,' I replied, although I'd never really thought about it. We met secretly on a wet Friday in March and sat and talked about the life of Arnold Pashley the sous chef from Brisbane and the sweaty realities of restaurant life. In the end, I thought, there was not much you could say because, when all was said and done he was just another gay Australian with a coke habit. We drank Trockenbeerenauslese with small pieces of Foie Gras and a brace of filleted fowl perched on bread fried in bacon fat. From time to time Harriet looked at me with her wet eyes and smiled.

Her father was a Marseillaise, her mother a Yamazat from Mandalay. Harriet's skin is gold and her hair shines blue-black in the white light of the restaurant. Perhaps she is slightly plump in certain places, but her eyes mesmerise me, and her mouth, like a rose in full bloom, forces the breath from my lungs. From time to time she takes a tin of balm from her bag and anoints her lips until her eyes and her mouth glitter like jewels. At three o'clock, we are drunk with wine and each other and I am tortured with the fear that she will leave; simply say goodbye and that I will never see her again. She stands and walks through the restaurant, glancing slyly over her shoulder. It is time to go and I have no idea what to say. When she returns, her face is taut and her hair is swept back and tied in a pony-tail. She takes her coat from the back of the chair, walks round the table, leans over me, slides her hot hand beneath my jacket and down between my legs and kisses me on the mouth.

Rain is bouncing off the pavement and the cab, when we climb in, smells vaguely of vomit. The open air and the wine have made me light-headed but Harriet's cheek is on my shoulder and after a while, her tongue is in my ear. The Kings Road traffic coagulates in the rain and we turn off into Roland Gardens and before I know it we are driving past Blakes and I have told the driver to stop and we are hurrying across the pavement and up the steps into the dry and the potted palms and cultured silence. The German girl at attention behind her desk wears a Tyrolean waistcoat and has her hair in a Dutt. She stares at Harriet who has collapsed into a velvet sofa, and I cough and say, 'We want a room now please.'

'Do you have any luggage?'

'No, we are carrying everything we could possibly need.'

'So. And how would you like to pay?' And I know it must be a slack day and we saunter down into the bar as if to prolong the anticipation of the cold cotton sheets against the heat of our naked skin.

But of course it is no good. There comes a time when your mind and your body are over-whelmed with desire and the scent of someone you hardly know becomes more than you can resist. We find the room down long silent corridors lit by low lamps. It overlooks a cobbled mews behind the hotel where we look down on silent passers by as they scurry past, leaning forward into the rain. Harriet asks room service to send up a bottle of Chateau Filhot and a cake.

In the bed she lies on her side, her knees up to her chin, her eyes on me as I fumble my clothes away and climb in beside her, the cotton sheets roaring as I stretch my legs.

'Are you going to fuck me?' she asks and I run my fingers down her spine, between her buttocks to the slippery wound of her pussy and she straightens and arches her body so that we are bound together from our mouths to our feet and I feel that fiery heat in my groin and my cock is like an iron rod and inflamed with hot blood and her cool hand is around it and she stares into my eyes as if she is about to cry out in pain and she brings her legs up around my waist and I am inside her and our coupling is brutal and loud and we are awash with sweat and the slick balm of our passion and when I come, she drags the fluid essence from me into the wet well of her belly.

Suddenly the room is full of sound. Through the walls, I can hear the muted, echoing cries of a woman delirious with passion, a Hoover whines somewhere in the distance and a waiting taxi idles in the mews. And so we lie for a while and consider what we have done.

'I don't think we should meet again,' she says as she stands by the bed and pulls her pants up into the sacred cleft of her bottom, 'this has been a terrible mistake.' And so I take her home and leave her standing, forlorn and tragic at the East end of Cambridge Gardens.

Two days later, we met in the late afternoon at The Flanker, a sports bar lodged somewhere between the Kensington sewers and the pavement. She drinks a Margarita and tells me that her lover, Craig, a New Zealander who knows all there is to know about cocktails, will be home for dinner and that she has no more than a few minutes. We make love in the echoing chambers of the men's lavatory, almost oblivious to the arrival of a party of rugby players on their way to Shepherds Bush. Against a background of farmyard noise she stretches her legs apart as she sucks me into her mouth, her naked calf around my waist, her bottom hard against the locked door and my hand in the hot, rustling folds of her groin, and while I am breathless from the fear and tension of discovery, I lose control and spill my seed into her throat while she smiles up into my eyes, and I look down at her chin slick with my come and feel her dexterous tongue lying like an eel alongside my shrinking, capitulating cock.

Our affair, such as it was, progressed in brief, juddering spurts of passion followed by periods of languid hauteur at the end of which one or other of us would phone and we would meet for some non-committal reason and start all over again. Sometimes she would make me thrash her, bending over the end of a bed and lifting her skirt, 'I want you to hurt me,' she would demand and after I had reduced her to tears and her buttocks were red raw, she would impale herself on me, her head thrown back, her eyes closed, screaming as she convulsed above me. Her mood would swing from quiet and submissive to violent, her expression turn to a cold fury as she clawed at my throat or hit me with her fists. She loved the thrill of love in public places or in her bed when Craig was on his way home from work. One hot summer afternoon she showed me her secret jewellery, a cigar box packed with crystals of crack which she would burn and smoke through tobacco and weed.

Later that summer as the city began to empty, I went to meet her at The Boulevard at the private time late at night when the guests have left and the staff can stretch their backs and put their feet up. She sat at the bar, sullen and quiet while the girls collected their tip money, the crisp notes neatly tucked into bulging brown envelopes all neatly arranged by the till.

'You knew nothing about Arnie, did you?' she said when I sat down. 'We all loved him. He knew how to make me happier than you ever could.' She walked behind the bar and poured herself a drink. 'He was always here for us, kept us going.' She came slowly back and put her hand on my shoulder, pulling me round so that I was facing her. The staff stopped chattering and turned to stare at us, Harriet stalking around me, looking up into my face from half-closed eyes, taking a lock of my hair between her fingers, tugging it sharply, leaning over and kissing me on the mouth. I should have walked out but I couldn't move. She laughed, sat on one of the stools by the bar. 'Arnie might be dead but he remembered us in his will,' she said and produced her little rucksack and laid it on the bar.

There is a glass wall at Boulevard, which stretches from floor to ceiling along the length of the restaurant. Within ten minutes the blinds had been pulled along the wall, the door locked and the first of the powder laid like a trail down the glass topped bar. Gopul handed round stubby little candy striped straws and one at a time we stretched forward and came up, eyes misty, lungs heaving, mouths paralysed. This was a regular event, I thought, plenty of cash and bags of Charlie. When I left, miserable with paranoia and chemically-induced dread, the dawn had started to wash away at the rim of night above Hyde Park. I wandered along Ladbroke Grove, relieved to be alone in the empty city and wondering about the life I was leading, wanting to get away but unable to do anything about it. I walked down Camden Hill across to Church Street and sat in a patisserie with a coffee until I felt that I could face the sordid reality of the paper. The news room was empty when I walked in, crumpled copies of yesterday's editions strewn around the desks and *Sky News* flickering silently on the television above the back bench. I sat and looked at the light flashing on my telephone and opened my emails from the Yard press office.

The Operation, code named *Crackerjack*, had been carried out at six am. 'Police and customs officers have this morning simultaneously raided addresses throughout West London and South Wales and 49 people have been arrested. No charges are expected until later in the day. The raids are in connection with the organised importation of huge quantities of class A drugs into the United Kingdom.' The release was timed at seven am.

I called Harriet and the phone was picked up immediately.

'Who is this calling?' Flat voice, estuary accent; unmistakable plod. I cut the connection, dialed my man in Notting Hill. 'Sorry son,' he said, 'You've heard, I suppose?' 'No, I've heard nothing.' 'Well, they busted your girlfriend this morning. Six o'clock.' It was as if I'd been hit in the chest. 'Dealing or importation?' I asked. 'She's been dealing all right,' he said, 'but this is a murder investigation. They found traces of Arnold Pashley's blood on her car. We think she did him on her night off. Some dispute over crack.'

Caught In A Storm

Slattery sat in his car and stared across the street. The gallery was packed for a mid-summer private view; guests spilling out on to the pavement, crop-haired men in black sweat-shirts under black jackets and women on the make, glasses in their hands, a babble of chatter. He looked through the crowd at the table inside the door, at the girl talking to an elderly man with a stumpy ponytail and writing something in a book, holding her dark hair away from her face while she wrote, the man glancing down the gap in her jacket. She was tall, slim, a touch of her Puerto Rican blood in the full mouth and tilted eyes. Slattery glanced at the file which lay open on his lap: Catherine McCall, aged 28, living alone in Sloane Avenue Mansions and paying rent of £750 per week. Caribbean mother, Scottish father. Her income from the gallery was probably no more than £25,000 a year. He wondered if she turned the occasional trick to boost her bank balance. He parked the car and crossed the Street. She glanced up at him standing by the desk as he said 'Good evening', handing her his business card which read CALLUM SLATTERY INSURANCE INVESTIGATORS. 'Do you have an invitation?' she asked, and he told her no, but he would welcome a few minutes of her time, when she was a little less occupied. She looked again at the card: 'I'm sorry, are you from the insurance company?' And he said: 'No, but they use me to deal with claims now and again. Nothing serious,' Slattery smiled reassuringly. 'Just a couple of odds and ends.' They arranged to meet at her flat at ten the following morning and he left thinking that the girl reminded him of someone, although he couldn't remember who.

Later, when the caterers had packed up and the last journalist had been kicked out and told to go home, Catherine wandered down Kinnerton Street and sat alone in Motcombs with a coffee and a glass of Sekt. She thought about Slattery and the way he looked in his charcoal suit. It had been four weeks since the insurance claim: £250,000 for a folio of Stanley Spencer sketches stolen from her car. It had been a collection of 25 nudes of the lesbian Patricia Preece who Spencer disastrously married in 1937. Catherine had acquired them from Elizabeth Ellis, who made a living renovating Romany caravans in Cookham. Catherine knew that the provenance was dodgy, no more than a letter from Spencer to the gallery owner Dudley Tooth, dated 20 March 1938. 'Any possibility of an advance?' he had written, 'I have made some studies of Mrs. Preece and I wish to intersperse them with some of the serious work.' The letter was genuine and came with the sketches, but Catherine knew it proved little. The dealer from Jenks of Bruton Place had finally signed the valuation halfway through a long and messy blowjob.

She lit a cigarette and eyed a weasely little man in a Hackett suit sitting at the bar reading *The Racing Post*. 'Jockey,' she decided, a profession she knew she could rely on for a bit of cash. She opened her handbag and removed a mirror. The man looked at her and smiled. It was dawn when she finally got rid of him. She had recognised his face from the sports pages and tied him down by suggesting brightly that she could drive down to Lambourne sometime and meet him in the Malt Shovel for a drink. All he'd wanted was to ejaculate over her tits. In the end he had managed it four times and it had taken six hours and she'd made him pay £250 a squirt. It was astonishing how small men were drawn to breasts, she thought, as she scrubbed herself in the shower before sitting on the stool in front of her mirror to anoint her pussy.

It was a daily ritual, washing and cleaning her vulva, trimming the hair, opening herself up with her fingers and delighting in the contrast of the coral pink of her vagina with the dark brown lips and golden skin of her groin. She would place her heels on the table beneath the mirror, bend her knees and slowly masturbate while she looked into the depths of her own eyes reflected in the glass. Sometimes the fluid would overflow onto her thighs and she would inhale her own potent scent. She reveled in the knowledge that it was an exercise in self-love. There was no one else in her mind as she worked away and listened to the liquid whispers of the moistened folds of skin and sinew.

~

Slattery arrived at her flat five minutes late and stood with his coffee looking down at Sloane Avenue five floors below. 'It's interesting,' he said, 'that six of the sketches were of Patricia naked on Cockmarsh Hill, yet Stanley never actually painted her nude in the open air. Tell me about the woman who sold them to you.' He turned and sat beside her on the long rose-coloured sofa. 'Lizzie still lives in Cookham,' she said, 'she used to run the Spencer Gallery in the village. There's nothing she doesn't know about Stanley, why don't you talk to her?' And she leant across, brushing his thigh with the sleeve of her dress, picking up the phone and prodding the numbers with a forefinger. 'Lizzie,' she said, after a while, 'there's a Mr.

Slattery here to talk to you. He's a private dick and he wants to know about Stanley's sketches of Patricia.' She handed him the handset and sank back into the sofa.

~

And so it came about that at eleven o'clock on a hot summer morning Catherine was in Slattery's old Saab convertible driving down the M4, turning off at Maidenhead and cutting across through the narrow lanes lined now with executive houses and their geometric gardens. Elizabeth had agreed to meet them on Cockmarsh Hill. 'She's getting on a bit now,' said Catherine. 'Stanley painted her as a child for *Love On The Moor.*' Cockmarsh stretches from Cookham Deane along the top of the escarpment, above the once beautiful valley where the Thames snakes down from Oxford through Henley and Marlow before voiding into the east. It is protected common land, a landscape of rough pasture, scrub and woodland, where, in high summer, skylarks whistle and slide high above the harebells and cowslips which Spencer came to paint while Mrs Preece slept on the grassy slope. In the dusk, lovers bewitched by the faint evocation of a lost rural Utopia and the shadows of owls quartering the fields, still come to Cockmarsh to stroll hand-in-hand and lie together in the soft grass.

Slattery parked and they walked to the crest of the slope and stared down towards the Thames far below. The emerald beech woods on Winter Hill sighed in the warm breeze and Slattery watched a pair of swans fly slowly along the river. They walked a little way down and sat in the thick grass. She said: 'What do you want to know?' 'Well, I want to know that the sketches were genuine and that they were stolen from your car when it was broken in to.' 'OK,' she said, 'you've got the valuation and copies of the drawings and I presume you've talked to the police. Shall I tell you what I want to know?' He looked at her, and she said: 'How long is the insurance company going to carry on getting on my tits, sending out loss adjustors and detectives and putting me off instead of settling the claim?' They sat for a while, not talking, Slattery suddenly remembering who she reminded him of as he looked at her sitting behind him, with her legs up and her skirt riding up her thighs. He said: 'You make me think of Rita Moreno.' And watched her as she sighed and lay back on the grass.

He had no idea how or why it happened. Perhaps it was the unaccustomed heat that sapped his resolve, or simple romantic weakness, but he decided for the first time, against his instinct and all his training, that he couldn't be bothered. It seemed to him inconceivable that he should pursue this girl. He knew that her claim was fraudulent, but it would be difficult to prove and, anyway, he didn't really care. He stood, slipped off his jacket and loosened his tie. She looked up at him, shading her eyes in the sunlight. He knelt beside her, passed his arm beneath her waist and lifted her and kissed her upturned face. Catherine, startled and assuming that Slattery's behaviour was the price she must pay to make his suspicion go away, encircled his legs with her arms and pulled him to the ground beside her. This was home territory, she thought, as she dragged her body onto him, her thighs between his, her hands inside his shirt, smothering him with her mouth, beginning to dismantle him, unbuckling his belt, biting his ear, and after a time, while girls trotted their ponies along the crest of the hill and Elizabeth Ellis waited patiently on a bench by the road and read her *Daily Mail*, began that timeless, unstoppable procedure, which always leads to trouble.

At midday a small weather front which had drifted whimsically across the valley bounced on the escarpment and unloaded its soft, warm rain onto the hot hillside. It was one of those sudden, violent summer storms which sometimes arrive in a heat wave and it came thundering without warning onto Catherine's back, soaking her dress, running into the channels of her neck, along her spine, between her buttocks, drenching her legs. Slattery, beneath her, his hand on her breast, his cock solid as a piano leg, was soaked in an instant. He felt the power of the water cracking like shrapnel on his back as he rolled on top of her, pulling at her clothes, dragging her dress over her shoulders, holding her thighs, pushing them apart and pausing to look at her face. Her eyes half closed, hands scrabbling at her pants and pushing them away in the grass while Slattery, breathless, his heart thudding like a hammer, pushed his cock along her sodden, sweet-scented groin and drove it slowly into the depths of her cunt as she groaned and closed her eyes.

It was not long before the white curtains of summer rain drumming on their bodies seemed to have stripped them bare and they were naked and shining like seals, hidden in their own grassy hollow deep in the hillside. Catherine's limbs were thrown out like a star and the muddy, wiry, muscular man moved relentlessly on her body, the skin of her shoulder in his mouth, clothes abandoned about them as they struggled and gasped in their hidden world. Somewhere in her consciousness, Catherine began to understand that this was no ordinary john and that what was happening to her had nothing to do with trade, and she abandoned herself to him, her breath hissing through clenched teeth, her hands in the valley of his groin, her finger sharp in his rectum, while he thrust into her. Callum felt that there were no limits of time or behaviour, and he turned her over and saw the water streaming off her back, his hand beneath her belly, as she opened her legs and bent her back letting him raise himself and take her perfect, wrinkled little anus and slowly force himself into her as she cried out and gave herself completely for the first time.

Twenty minutes later the storm had rumbled away towards Bourne End, leaving the hillside steaming in the sunlight. Birds reappeared from the dripping woods filling the air with chatter. Catherine and Callum, feeling the heat on their skin once more, lay on their sides, murmuring quietly to each other as they moved, their bodies entwined slick with sweat and rain. Slattery, moving slowly and rhythmically inside her while her mouth was on him, her tongue like a snake and he smiled and asked if she was ready as he abandoned control over that tense complicated muscle and flooded into her with his pent up, heartfelt wash.

They emerged from Cockmarsh flecked with mud, hair plastered on their faces, drenched, their clothes baggy and covered in grass. Elizabeth Ellis watched them as she sat on the bench beneath her umbrella, which was now providing shelter from the sun. She thought how Spencer would have loved to paint them. He would have appreciated the untidiness, the dirty faces and the way they held each other like lovers.

'Hello Lizzie,' said Catherine, 'I'm afraid we've brought you out on a bit of a wild goose chase.' Slattery shook her hand. 'Yes, and I'm sorry we're late,' he said. 'Got caught in the rain.' He sat down, plucked a cornflower from the verge and gave it to Catherine. 'Let's go down to the Black Dog,' he suggested. 'I'm sure we could all do with a drink.'

I know something is stirring as soon as I walk into court. I can sense it in the faces of the jury with their eyes focused on the witness box. Something has made them sit up. I look at the Bench, graced today by her ladyship Judge Winifred Bone. She is leaning slightly to her left, eyes closed, wide awake. In the dock stands Cutler, tall, bony, shaved head, hands on the parapet. Beneath him, in the crowded benches of the well, I see Virginia Massey, slim and exquisite, wig tipped slightly forward, gown slipping off a shoulder, glasses on the tip of her nose, one hand behind her back.

Then I hear the words and know what has entranced them: a voice almost more beautiful than true, coming from between familiar lips in a face now obscured by the high dock. It is a woman's voice, soft and clear and utterly persuasive: 'I met him at a Midsummer reception in the Royal Academy in 1999. Someone introduced him as a Director of nineteenth-century paintings at Christie's. I liked him, he seemed detached, unworldly.'

I move forward onto a bench below the jury where I can see the witness box. And there she is, Catherine Church, standing to attention with her head slightly back, hair pulled away from her black, oval face and tied in a pony-tail. I see once again those prominent, slanted eyes, angled over high cheekbones and a mouth round and generous with a line of pink, soft skin where the lips come together.

Virginia Massey turns to look at the jury. 'Miss Church, please tell the court what happened on the night you met Mr. Cutler.' Catherine looks down at her hands and then, briefly, at the man in the dock.

'Well,' she says, 'as we walked round the galleries, he talked about a painting by Joseph Turner known as *Charing Cross by Moonlight*. He went on about the light and the pigmentation and he told me how Turner had lived in a tavern called The Ship and Bladebone in Limehouse Reach before he changed his name to Booth and died in a boarding house in Cheyne Walk. He said, we must go down to Charing Cross right away and look at the moonlight, and then he said, "I will drive you to Limehouse."'

Catherine pauses and looks apologetically at the jury. 'It might sound strange, but I quite appreciate this sort of rubbish. It was so corny and he was very intense about it all. He spoke as if he had been born in another age and said he was only interested in the past. He took me to the courtyard where he had parked his Lagonda and opened the door and tucked me in before we set off into Piccadilly; he was very courteous.'

'And did you drive to Charing Cross?'

'Oh yes, and we looked at the river in the moonlight and he held my hand and then we sped away down the embankment towards the East End. After we came to Wapping, he turned off the Commercial Road and parked in a street leading down to the river by the Limehouse Basin. Cutler said it used to be called the Ratcliffe Highway and that Turner's lodgings had been round the corner. He told me that this was once a stretch of marshland where the murderer John Williams killed a mother and father and two children. He attacked them with a hammer and then slit their throats, then he did the same thing to another family twelve days later. They executed Williams in 1812 when Turner lived here and before they tossed his corpse into the lime pit in front of Wapping Church, they drove a stake through his heart.'

Catherine's voice, confident and slightly contemptuous, seems to fill the court. No one has any doubt that what she is saying is true, and the melodious lilt of her speech charms everyone who is listening. Of course I am familiar with that voice. There have been times when just a word or two spoken on the telephone would immediately enslave me. I know, in spite of what she is saying, that Cutler was already captivated on the night he drove her to Limehouse. He would have lost his control seconds after meeting her. It is a power which she can use at will.

Catherine has stopped speaking and is waiting for a cue from counsel. 'Can you explain why Cutler would have raised so gruesome a subject on such an occasion?' 'I think he was at a loss about what to say. He wanted to seduce me, but his nerve failed and he resorted to a lurid story.'

'So what did he do?' Catherine looks across to the dock and is silent for a moment before turning and glancing at the judge. 'He climbed out of the car and took my arm. "Come with me," he said, "I have something to show you." We crossed the road to a derelict warehouse on the bank of the river. He unlocked the metal door and I followed him into a wire cage lift which took us to the top of the building.' 'And what did you find there?'

'It was a large room, a studio which took up the whole of one floor. The far wall was glazed and I could see Southwark spread out to the south and the river winding away down to Greenwich. He switched on some ceiling lamps, which flooded the room and the brick walls in a brilliant white glare. "This is where I work," he said. The studio was almost bare; an unmade, old-fashioned hospital bed, table, stereo, canvasses in piles or leaning against the walls, an easel covered in a blanket by the window, a smell of turpentine and paint.' Virginia Massey shuffles her notes and looks up at the witness box. 'Did you feel threatened in any way?'

'In a sense I did, yes; after all, I was alone with a man I had only just met. I walked to the window and looked down at the river and he followed me and put his hands on my shoulders. I knew what he wanted to do.'

'And what was that?'

'He wanted to fuck me.' There is a silence. Catherine, cool and relaxed is staring at the jury who, as one, are now looking at their hands, unable to raise their heads and risk catching her eye. She twists the knife. 'Actually, I liked the idea of being fucked up there in full view of a million people.'

There is a dry cough from the bench and her ladyship Judge Winifred Bone opens her eyes and leans towards counsel. 'What is the relevance of this evidence?' Virginia Massey appears irritated at the interruption. 'It is the Crown's case that the defendant was incapable of rational judgment and that Miss Church had to gain complete control over him. In my submission, her recollection of these events is significant.' She turns once more to the witness box. 'I repeat, was Mr. Cutler's behavior in any way threatening?'

'Yes, I suppose it was. His voice had changed and his grip was harder than it needed to be. He wanted to be in control of me.' 'How did you respond?' 'I turned to him and said, "Not here Cutler," and I led him across the room, keeping my eyes on his face. We knelt on the bed and I put my arm around his shoulders and kissed him.' 'How did he respond?' 'He turned his head and spat on the floor.' Catherine, composed, eyebrows slightly raised, waits patiently for the cross-examination to continue. 'Did he remain kneeling?' 'He tried to but I told him to lie down.' 'And did he?' 'Of course. Men generally do what I want when I ask them to, particularly in bed. He just lay down and I lay on top of him.' 'Why did you do this?' 'Because I wanted to control him. It is part of my job to carry restraints so I removed them from my handbag, pushed his right arm towards the bed head and handcuffed him to it.' I look at the jury whose heads are unanimously raised once again. 'Why did you handcuff him?' asks Virginia Massey. 'Because I wanted to search his studio.' 'How did he react?' 'He wound his left arm round me and pulled me down. I could feel his cock against my stomach and his mouth against my neck I decided to let him do what he wanted to me.'

'Why?' 'Because I felt he would be easier to manage afterwards.' And so Catherine launches into a vivid description of the 'calming down' of Greville Haslett Cutler RA; she explains how he had seemed to assume that the restraint was no more than a sexual ploy. 'He ignored it and brought his left hand up inside my dress and into my pants. He didn't seem to have the imagination to do anything else.' I see her glance once more at the dock: 'so I decided to take the initiative and undressed him as far as I could.' 'In other words, you removed his trousers?' 'Yes. And then I stood up and removed my skirt and my knickers and, keeping my eyes fixed on his, draped them across the easel by the window. He lay there watching me, knowing that there was nothing he could do until I released him. His erection appeared to have matured and was now impossible to ignore. I decided that it would be sensible to deal with it straight away, just to keep him calm, so I arranged myself on the bed facing the window, opened my legs so that my private parts were over his face and took his cock in my mouth.' I can see immediately that this is too much for her Ladyship Judge Winifred Bone, not to mention the jury, judge's clerk, court typist, lady usher and defense counsel, all of whom are unsuccessfully doing their best to convey expressions of studied unconcern. 'Miss Church, I am not convinced that any of this is relevant. You must confine your evidence to the facts. The details of an alleged sexual encounter with the defendant do not, it seems to me, fall into this category.' Catherine, unfazed, raises her eyebrows and looks expectantly at Victoria Massey who, turning wearily to the judge, says, 'With the greatest respect, your ladyship, Miss Church's experiences in the defendant's studio are central to the Crown case, and we are almost there.' Judge Bone, wary, sits back in silence. Catherine, turning once again towards the jury, continues, 'In my opinion, Mr. Cutler was extremely tense. I took his cock in my mouth for possibly two minutes before moving and sitting across his lap so that he could enter me. As he did so, I took the second set of restraints from my bag, leant forward and shackled his left ankle to the bottom of the bed. As I did so, he ejaculated inside me.' The courtroom is silent. The jury is drenched in post-coital calm.

Catherine pauses to take a sip of water. 'I left the bed and tidied myself up. Cutler seemed relaxed, but had probably started to realise what was going on. Then I reached for my skirt and as I did so lifted the blanket off the painting easel. And there it was, where I knew it would be. *Charing Cross By Moonlight*, painted by Joseph Mallord William Turner in 1797 and stolen from Lord Winstone's Ballroom at Langley House in 1997, 200 years after it was painted. It was all over. I sat on the studio floor with my back to the window and lit cigarettes for Cutler and myself. After a while, he said in a low voice. "You work for the insurance."'

'I sat there until the sky in the east turned pink and I could hear the dawn birdsong and the traffic rumbling again on the Commercial Road. Then I took Cutler's car keys and the painting and went. I left my knickers hanging on the easel to give him something to remember me by.'

'Did he speak to you, before you left?'

'Yes, as I walked out of the door, he said, "The Sun is God."'

UNCLE ARCHIE

My Friend Archie was a millionaire many times over. It was inherited wealth. His father was something big in tinned meat, and tight as a tourniquet. The old man had come up the hard way, born in a bothy and abandoned at the farm gate, but now he lived in a castle near Inverness, Lord of all he surveyed, luxuriating in the status of local Worthy and Elder of the Kirk. One raw winter night, when Archie was eight, his father sent the staff home and took the boy to the kitchen where he lectured him soundly about the evils of the flesh. Candlelight flickered on the walls and on the pack of cards, the whisky and the leather-bound edition of the poetical works of Burns which was lying on the old, scrubbed table.

One by one these symbols of the decadence of humanity were cast into the open door of the range which had been stoked up for the occasion. The final projectile, a triangular bottle of Grants Standfast, detonated dramatically and showered the flagstone floor with burning embers. Archie was then sent to Gordonstoun and flogged mercilessly every day until he left ten years later at the age of eighteen.

The gothic scene in the castle kitchen left a lasting impression on the young boy. On leaving school and pocketing a generous allowance prior to going down to University, he made his way to Chelsea, got laid, learned to snort cocaine and gamble heavily at backgammon in the Clermont Club. When he was twenty his father died and Archie bought a house in Chelsea Square from where he did his best to fuck his way through the West End.

Society looked on indulgently until, two years after leaving school, he crashed his Aston Martin into a police car in Ebury Street having lost control as he ejaculated sumptuously into the mouth of a pretty Swedish prostitute called Flottie who had been sucking his cock since the Vauxhall Bridge Road.

He was an adventurous lover, probably because he nearly always paid for sex and could thus indulge his fantasies. The scars of his childhood meant that the emotional demands of real live girls were beyond him. Alone on his twentieth birthday he trussed up and gagged an impecunious Australian nurse following elaborate guidelines from a German bondage manual. Having exhausted all the cord and rope in the house, he went next door to borrow a short length of string with which to bind her thumbs. His return coincided with the arrival at the front door of eight members of the London Scottish Rugby club, one of whom, an acquaintance from school, announced that he had come to show Archie's beautiful house to his teammates, before bursting through the front door and staggering upstairs. The boy's reputation blossomed from that moment and his 'debauched dinners' were always well attended.

His housekeeper, Mrs Collins, once told me that she had found an unconscious girl behind the sofa in the morning room when she was cleaning up after a party. 'The poor child had a cucumber up her bottom,' she remarked indulgently. 'So I removed it and put her to bed.'

⌒

One year in early summer, Archie decided to spend a month in the Cyclades and chartered a 65-foot ketch called *La Belle*

Epoque. He asked me along because he wanted someone to drink with and keep him amused. We arrived in Piraeus where I was given a bunk amidships while he took the aft cabin. He had arranged to fly out a number of women who would join us one at a time at various islands.

The first was called Jenny and I soon realised that he had never actually seen her in daylight. 'I met her at Annabel's,' he said. 'She's insane. You can fuck her whenever you want. We'll tie her to the mast. She'll love it.' Jenny turned out to be a six-foot-tall pasty woman with big feet and a sniffle, but Archie was quite happy and, throughout the night, the marina was electrified with the sounds of her screams accompanied by Archie's animal bellowing drifting across the still water. Nobody slept and the skipper was livid.

When we were moored in Hydra two days later, Jenny lay on a lump of tar on the beach and then came back and sat on the wooden deck. It was too much and she was sent home in disgrace. 'My deck is an altar,' said the skipper, a mantra he repeated to all who came aboard.

We had reached Kea when the second guest, an Irish nymph called Siobhan with pale green eyes and black hair, arrived on a ferry. Archie immediately stole her passport, 'because she looks like a bolter,' and we set sail for a remote island romantically named Syphnos by the skipper. Siobhan, a folk singer from County Kerry who had been unfortunate enough to succumb to Archie's persuasive charms in Motcomb's, refused to cooperate with his sleeping arrangements and spent the night alone on deck beneath the stars.

She seemed remote and looked the other way when the next morning Archie suggested coarsely that, as a penance, she should strip off and bend over the stern while we all had our way with her. The Skipper smirked but I caught her eye and shrugged sympathetically. After a long lunch of salad and retzina in the well of the boat we took the *Zodiac* to water ski in a nearby bay. Siobhan stayed behind alone.

The skiing trip faltered after Archie's false front teeth, a legacy of his violent school life, shot from his mouth during a tricky slalom, leaving him with a top jaw gaping from canine to canine. We could see the teeth lying on the bottom in the clear water, about thirty feet down and too deep for me to dive. Archie told the skipper that he was not going back to the boat without his dentures and someone had to go down for them or fish them out on a line. After fifteen minutes of fruitless effort, I swam back to *La Belle Epoque*.

I climbed aboard and lay in the bows; my head on a biscuit and my shorts tied to a shroud. Siobhan was motionless on the cabin roof, a floppy hat across her face. The sun was a dull glow through my eyelids, the only sound the slapping of the sea on the hull and the creaking of the rigging. After a while, I heard her moving, she was behind me, slipping softly along the deck, pulling herself towards me on her stomach. I lay motionless; then I felt her fingers on my lips and I knew that she was on her stomach, her head touching mine, her other hand in my hair, gently pulling. I felt her tongue licking the salt from my ear, her teeth on the lobe. She did not speak.

I put my hands palm down on the deck, slowly bent my knees and brought my legs back over my head placing my feet softly down on either side of her waist. She was naked. I slid backwards and lay gently on top of her, my cock between the cheeks of her bottom. She said nothing but slowly moved her feet apart on the deck and brought her arm up behind her to hold the nape of my neck. I felt the swell of her buttocks beneath me and smelled her musky scent on the still air. She raised the middle of her body, her breasts flat on the deck, arching the small of her back.

I entered her and felt the wet heat of her and looked down and saw her spread before me, her little wrinkled sphincter opening and closing like a sea anemone as I thrust into her. I touched the faint, soft down at the base of her spine. She said nothing. I held her black hair in my hand and brought her head up and back as I moved inside her. I was in another country. I beat her on the buttocks with my hand, leaving scarlet prints on her white flesh. She said nothing.

Then she turned over and pulled me down to her red mouth, locked her legs about my waist and found my cock with a twist of her pelvis. Time stood still until I heard the sound of the *Zodiac* in the distance but before I could melt and spill into her she sat up, took my cock from inside her and moved behind me so that she was holding my balls in her left hand and gently masturbating me with her right.

When I came it was as if I was spending my very essence into the air and on to the pristine white deck. She said nothing, but worked her way around me, and lay before me, legs apart, her hand wiping the creamy secretions from her pussy. Then she leant forward and, with her fingers, shaped my come mixed with hers into the form of a heart on the holy, white teak. Then she leant forward and kissed me.

By the time Archie and the skipper were back on board, the juicy product of our union had dried in the sun and left an unmistakable and indelible symbol on the apex of the foredeck. I believe it's still there.

Salad Days

I was around fourteen, I suppose, already a veteran of five years in a monastery-run public school and I was taking a pee in the lavatory next to the senior common room. It was three in the afternoon and the school was at sports – out in the February cold and wet, playing rugby or scampering aimlessly about in the all-pervading mud. The priests were in their cells, masturbating or chewing sweets or whatever they did in the afternoons. I was alone, miserable as usual, playing a stream of urine up and down the grey cement. The door opened and Dru came in. A popular boy, clever, maybe a year older than I, with short, fair hair. He settled himself before the wall, unbuttoned his fly and started to urinate. He stood close to me and said, 'Do you like Glynis Johns?' We wore grey suits, grey shirts and thin school ties patterned with diagonal stripes of blue, red and gold. The band of gold was thinner than the other two colours. I suspected it represented a rich vein of something precious; knowledge maybe, or the love of God.

Dru reached into his pocket and removed a folded page torn from a magazine. He opened it out, using both hands, and held it against the tiled wall above the urinal. I noticed that his cock was still protruding from his trousers. It was elegant and slim, uncircumcised, the foreskin long, longer than mine, anyway. He was a handsome boy, Dru, with a high forehead and eyes set wide apart. I looked at the picture. Glynis was standing with her back to the camera, glancing over her shoulder and wearing white silk knickers. Her upper back was naked and one automatically presumed that her breasts were exposed, although, of course, this was the fifties when you could not expect to see even a hint of the precious, rounded flesh. But it was her lazy eyes which I loved, and her husky voice. I had seen her in *Miranda*, swimming deep below the surface of the sea, her long blonde hair always protecting her modesty. I knew where she lived with her second husband in Sunningdale. It was near my parents house and in the holidays I would sometimes cycle over and stand by the gate for a while, just to be near her. Dru began to read the caption; 'Where's me shirt?' he read, 'Glynis Johns, one of Britain's favourite actresses, still has time to pose for Lilliput in spite of her busy schedule. Last time we saw her playing a mermaid in her hit film *Miranda*, she was wearing a tail and nothing else. So we thought our readers might like to be reminded that Glynis has lovely legs as well.'

As he finished speaking the words, giving a little groan as he did so, he folded the page, leant over and gently took my cock in his hand. He stared at it for a moment and said, 'That's nice.' He started to slip his hand up and down the stiffening flesh and said, 'You can hold mine,' and so I reached down and took it between my thumb and forefinger. It was firm and hard and when I pulled the foreskin hack towards his body, the membrane slid stiffly over the head of his prick and revealed the pale, tender muscle beneath. No one but me had ever touched my cock and I had certainly never touched anyone else's. I became light headed and I could feel my heart pounding with fear. We looked down at what we were doing in the thunderous silence of the fetid little pissoir, half listening for the footsteps of an approaching monk, and half longing for the mysterious release which I had never known, and, as Dru gripped and pulled and panted through his mouth, I felt my body die for the first time, helpless and out of control of my will and my consciousness and as I came, I felt through my fingers the spontaneous, swelling current of his own ejaculation, and I watched as it burst from him, a molten broth of whipped milk, onto my wrist and over his clothes, while my breath was forced from my lungs. And I thought that what we had done was not merely the result of sexual desire, it was a pure and honourable expression of defiance.

The priest, Petroc, arrived a moment too late; silent on furtive, crepe-soled feet, his head round the door; suspicious, his soft voice demanding why we were here and not freezing to death outside and I said that the matron had given me a note and that she had excused me from games and Dru, in his confusion, mumbled, 'She's excused me too, Father.'

~

That night, Petroc came to the dormitory and took Dru from his bed and flogged him for lying. Thirty boys were installed like convicts in their cubicles. Our doors shut, our faces ablaze as we listened to our friend screaming and begging the priest for mercy. And afterwards we lay there while he wept and choked himself into miserable silence. I thought that if I'd had a club I would have walked from my cell and struck the priest with all my strength. I could have swung the weapon into his kidneys and when he was down, I would have broken his right elbow and then his wrist. And because I also wanted to see his blood, I would have stamped on his face and broken his nose and dismantled his mouth. I would have forced him to crawl before me along the floor and, as he reached the door of that long, miserable chamber, I would have swung my club at the base of his spine and taken his cane and snapped it and pushed the pieces past his broken teeth. Even now, fifty years later with Petroc long dead, my hatred of him and his brethren is like a cancer in my gut.

~

That summer I met Elizabeth Rhys-Jones on the hot, white sands of Damer Bay. She was like a fresh shoot of asparagus I thought, full of juice and firm as a bicep. She emerged from the surf in the blue woollen costume and white rubber bathing hat which her mother forced her to wear in a vain attempt to protect her by blunting her natural beauty. As a stratagem it had been unsuccessful. When she pulled the hat from her head, I saw that her tumbling hair had started to turn gold from the sun and the wind and that there was a light dusting of salt on her cheeks and around her mouth. Her eyelashes, seen from the side, were thick and curved, her eyes a grey-blue and her mouth generous and tucked upwards at the corners. Her teeth were white as the crest of a wave on a sunny day. She moved unaffectedly, kicking her heels in the sand, her body lightly muscled below slim shoulders, and her legs, my God. Oh, she was perfect but, as I got to know her, I realised that the most perfect thing about her was that she had absolutely no concept of her own beauty.

When, after days of fragmentary and halting conversation, we met secretly in the dunes at night, her kisses were dry and salty, and when we fumbled with each other, she showed no reserve, just accepted what I did and when at last I touched her silken pussy with my mouth, she leant forward to watch and pulled herself apart with her long brown fingers. During the four short days we had together, we did not leave each other alone and every moment apart was unendurable. At night we would swim naked, wondering at the flecks of sparkling phosphorus which streamed from our fingertips in the pure sea, and we would embrace, standing, battered by the surf, my cock like a hot ember on her stomach and her breasts pressed hard against my weedy little chest. She was a virgin. 'We must wait,' she said in her Home Counties way, 'after all, I'm only thirteen and I think it would be best to hang on until I am a little older,' but she happily accepted all I would do to her with my fingers in her pretty, wrinkled little anus and my tongue in the folds of flesh around her clitoris. Sometimes we would lie in the dunes on beds of clover and thyme and when she knew that I was about to come she would take me in her hand while I disintegrated over her breasts and into the soft hollows of her neck and in the early morning we would creep back to our beds, our bodies caked with sand and our hearts full of longing.

Late in the Christmas term, I described it all to Dru, and let him read her letters as we sat together on his bed, feverishly pulling at each other's cocks after two months of celibacy. 'Did you do it?' he asked, 'Did you put it into her? Tell me everything.'

Elizabeth and I met again in the holidays before Christmas and I collected her from the train at Victoria Station and we took a bus and sat at a table with a chequered red and white oil-skin cloth in a bistro in South Kensington. Full of adolescent anxiety and unable to think of anything to say, we held hands and ate our spaghetti, . Afterwards we walked in the park and sat in the bandstand near Kensington Gardens and I kissed her and put my hand gently on her breast and she told me that that she would take my letters to bed and that after she had read them, she would sleep with them beneath her nightdress, next to her skin.

That spring, she came to stay with some cousin in Virginia Water and we went together to a party at the golf club. She wore a long blue taffeta dress with a stiff boned bodice and a string of pearls. Her mother had given her a pair of long calf skin gloves and she had borrowed someone's shoes with stiletto heels and there was lipstick, badly applied, and mascara and a dash of *Chanel*. But when I looked at her, I saw a girl, whose skin was perfumed with thyme and whose lips were flavoured with salt as she ran through the surf on a summer morning in Trebetherick. That night we found a bed at some friend's house on the estate and I remember standing behind her and holding her and putting my hands inside the stiff fabric of the dress and feeling her nipples rise beneath my fingers. She said, 'I want you to undress me,' and she watched while I fumbled at the zips and pulled the frock above her head, and beneath it she wore silk stockings and wonderful tight cotton knickers and when she was naked and I was staring helplessly at her, she took my hand and put it between her legs before, rather dramatically I felt, leading me to the bed and pulling me down on her, and I suppose nature took over, because I had no control over what I did. I remember the sudden pungent scent of her and the desperation as she took me in her hand and sucked at me until I was as rigid as it was possible to be without detonation, and her legs were around my waist and her saliva on my face and her cries in my ear, and I understood that the innocent young fawn I had met at on the sands at Damer

Bay had died, and when I entered her and she cried out and I came almost immediately and felt the viscous, bloody essence of our union on my legs, I knew that what had happened was a stratagem into which I had been recruited.

It was a lesson, I suppose, the first of many. Dru immediately understood when I told him. 'Women rule the world, baby,' he said, reaching inside my trousers. I never saw Elizabeth again, but then, I suppose, neither did anyone else.

Heavy Corsetry

My mother's underwear was made by Woods of Morecambe. I know this because when I was a small child, I used to sneak into her bedroom and take a look at the stiff, whale-boned brocade corsetry she kept in flat boxes in her chest of drawers. I used to sniff the garments to see whether I could detect some warm intimate scent which would perhaps tell me what had been going on in the bedroom.

I would examine them centimetre by centimetre, removing tiny, curled hairs and fragments of skin. I can remember the twirly 'W's on the boxes and the little silk labels carefully stitched in the back of the garments, the embroidered flowers and the lacing and the white, geometric, enamelled eyeholes. The suspenders with their little wire frames and rubber attachments especially beguiled me.

The complex engineering of corsetry was a fundamental part of my childhood now I come to think of it. I was aware from an early age that it was a science used by women, not just as away of generating a small waist, but as a form of warmth and security and, occasionally, a barrier against unwelcome attention from men. Because I was a child, the women I saw in their intimate moments were unrestrained, casually dismissing me as little more than a baby, a small, innocent being who had no concept of the complex science of a mature female's private being and no idea of what made her tick.

But I knew what was going on and I was developing a passion for the loins of those comfortable, well-endowed creatures who sometimes came to tea or who stayed to dinner and were invited to spend a night in the guest room. Sometimes, late at night, I would sneak along the landing and open the forbidden door, look through the clothes tumbled out of the suitcase, run my little hands through the silk, feel the stiffening in the strong fabric, the lightness of the nylon stockings and wonder why my heart was beating like a rabbit drumming its legs in alarm.

During the last war my mother and I avoided all the European unpleasantness by retiring tactfully to the Isle of Man. In the meantime, my father went to Egypt where he frightened the shit out of the Italian Army as a Captain in the Royal Dental Corps. Onchan, where we lived quietly in a genteel Edwardian villa and were waited on hand and foot by German prisoners of war, was probably the safest place in the world. Between 1940 and 1946, the entire island was a prisoner of war camp and consequently out of bounds to the Luftwaffe. But it was a bleak, lonely corner of the Union and when she was feeling desolate and alone, my mother would send off for some intimate garment or other and it would arrive a fortnight later carefully wrapped up in tissue and ribbon.

The Woods factory was in Morecambe and still is. They owned a shop on the promenade where my mother had once taken shelter during a windswept outing from Manchester University during the 1920s. She had unearthed a treasure trove of intimacy, wooden busts on small poles draped in cotton liberty bodices with cloth-covered buttons and suspenders; little wood-panelled changing rooms with long oval mirrors and signs asking ladies to ensure that they were as meticulous as possible when they were trying on new garments. 'Accounts to be settled within four weeks please.'

In those days there were corsetières in every town in England and foundation garments were worn whether you needed to hide the occasional bulge or whether you didn't. The amour-like rigidity of women's formal underwear in the post-war years was a reflection on the morals of the time and was more than a match for any randy matelot, however strong his fingers were.

Later, during the Fifties and Sixties, we saw the invasion of the pantyhose, a bandage-like tubular support which stuck to the skin like latex. It was dismissed by London youth as a moral defense technique developed by religious fundamentalists in the United States. The entry procedure was complicated and was the post-war feminist equivalent of the Enigma code. Once established *in situ*, the only practical way in which pantyhose could be removed was with vigorous and experienced physical effort by the person wearing them, and then only after a struggle. I once sprained my wrist in the course of removing a set of pantyhose from a girl called Suzie in the back of a Mini Cooper on Chobham Common.

Suzie was plump and beautiful, the daughter of a newspaper magnate. She had agreed to let me drive her home after a night out with the Young Conservatives and here we were struggling in the dark in the middle of the bleakest stretch of wasteland of southern England. We had broken the ice by indulging in a bout of vigorous, adolescent foreplay and the two front seats were down as far as they could go. The gear stick was in third which gave one a faint chance of getting one's loins in close proximity without severe injury. And the hand brake was off.

It was not as if there was any resistance from Suzie; her skirt was around her waist, her knickers were around her ankles, her Maiden-form bra was unhooked and she had managed to winkle out my hopelessly ill-disciplined and weedy little cock from its cotton nest and with impressive legerdemain and acrobatic dexterity had even managed to give it a brief suck. But, tragically, she was wearing pantyhose.

These things don't come under the classification of heavy corsetry; a trade description, certainly conceived by a woman married to an officer in the Royal Artillery. No, no, they were lightweight and designed theoretically to disguise a small, unsightly tummy bulge and reduce the visual impact of a large bottom. The trouble was that they were ETBs, a schoolgirl acronym for "elastic top and bottoms", and the US manufactured elastic was powerful enough to prohibit any downward movement by an outside agency.

Between us we managed, after a while, to pull them down a small way. As luck would have it, my right hand had become entangled in the waist-band of the pantyhose and as I tugged sharply downwards and moved backwards, the door of the Mini Cooper opened outwards and I fell from the seat into a ditch by the roadside, sharply twisting some joint in my wrist. Unfortunately, this sharp movement resulted in the gear lever returning to neutral and the car rolling slowly backwards, coming to a stop with the front wheels resting on my right knee.

Suzie told me later as she rubbed liniment into my bruised body, that she only wore pantyhose as a way of keeping warm. I didn't care, I loved them in spite of the injury they had caused. Personally, I think there is something extraordinarily sexy about a girl in pantyhose, particularly the 'Firm Control 18 hour in Spanette', as marketed by Woods of Morecambe.

The 'All In One' is the perfect restraint garment after all, and the tactile thrill of thrusting your hand down between the tight fabric and your lover's skin, and the brief exploration of that hidden, hot, hairy, nesty wetness before your arm becomes paralysed from lack of blood, is a uniquely British pleasure.

Predictably, by the Seventies, these sophisticated power knickers became unfashionable. Dismissed by impatient British youths as 'passion killers' they disappeared from the high street. But not at Woods of Morecambe who, thanks be to God, still sell the 'Firm Control 18 Hour Pantie Corselette' in Spanette fabric.

It is to be regretted that the provincial corsetière has become an endangered species in Britain; there aren't any in my local *Yellow Pages*. They have gone partly because the skills required to measure and fit these magnificent garments have vanished and the old shops have been replaced by lingerie outlets selling cheap, mass-produced knickers, bras, garter belts and stockings. Nowadays, most women don't feel the need to protect themselves with body amour while they are involved in normal social intercourse. They no longer go to tea dances or wear narrow waisted, formal dresses and the craftsmanship required to design and manufacture the sort of beautifully crafted heavy corsetry our grandparents wore has long since vanished.

Woods of Morecambe, however, have not just survived, they have prospered and still have available wonderful, figure-hugging garments like the 'Silhouette Open Corselette', a 'pull-on style with double panel for extra support with three-section soft cups, adjustable stretch shoulder straps and four suspenders.' Christ, you have to see it to appreciate the beauty of this great white nylon tube on the plump model with her soft, generous body, perfect hair, skin and teeth. But best of all they have kept the 'Fantasie Tweave Open Corselette. Light Control with its sheer half cup. Lightweight but a snug fit. Open style pull-on.' Just fill your mind with the tons of flesh which are even now crammed into delicious devices like this. Think of how they are put on in the morning; the rising from the warm bath, hot and pink, Tweed powder puff padded extravagantly over the buttocks and between the legs. Slip on the white cotton briefs, high on the stomach, severe, elasticated with double duty gusset. The Corselette is hanging in the cupboard, fresh from the wash, and carefully ironed; suspenders hanging like little traps ready to grip the top of a pair of grey Merino wool stockings with the added resilience of nylon and Lycra Elastane. Heaven.

Underwear for the masses has remained static since the Seventies in my opinion. According to the police, recorded incidences of theft involving clothing have reduced to almost zero since 2000. I am of course referring to theft of underwear from washing lines which was once classified as 'behaviour likely to cause a breach of the peace'. Flashing is now considered a serious crime, a type of indelicacy which behavioral psychologists believe can develop into seriously dysfunctional behavior if allowed to prosper. But stealing knickers from a back garden and taking them back to your bedsit for close examination seems a harmless peccadillo to me. Many of those who indulge in this fantasy will sit on their sofa in the evening with the garments slipped tightly over their heads, breathing in the scent of Comfort and Persil and, perhaps now and then, inhaling the delicious tang of something considerably more personal. Because it is the only way they will ever achieve intimate contact with the object of their affection. Fair enough, I suppose. God I love big women, and if you do too, go to the Woods website: www.woods-online.co.uk. And inhale deeply.

SICK

I AM CONSCIOUS and in a darkened room. I presume it is night-time; there is a dim glow from a lamp by the bed and I can see that the curtains are drawn. My mouth is open and my palate and tongue are dry. The corner of my mouth is moist and I have been dribbling on the pillow. The sheets are crisp and clean and drawn up to my chin and the bed is adjusted so that I am lying at a slight angle with my head and shoulders above the rest of me. I feel relieved for some reason; happy to be alive. There are flowers and a greeting card on the table by my bed. I turn my head slowly and I can see that the door of the room is open and that there is a soft light outside. I can hear a voice, calm and low, a woman, talking on the telephone.

A tube has been taped into the back of my hand. I feel no pain. I follow the tube with my eyes up to a bag of clear liquid hanging from a stand by the bed. It is coming back to me now. The shuffle along the thick, carpeted corridors to my room, unpacking, apprehensive, a pathetic attempt to shave myself in the bath. Vivid memories of Daisy, months ago taking a razor and trimming my pubic hair into a thin line up to my navel and laughing and taking me between her beautiful wet lips and running her tongue around the head of my cock and seeing her saliva all over my balls while I came in her hot, red, slippery mouth.

I recall the anesthetist sidling into the room, with the manner of an accountant. 'You'll just feel a tiny prick, then count to six.' Later, I was high on hospital heroin, waiting for the cutters to come for me, and then they were wheeling me down the corridor and there were women in green gowns standing around and the surgeon, Mr Bakewell, looking at his watch. That was all. Then, oblivion.

Now I am conscious again and I know they have carved great wounds into my groin and rummaged around inside my abdomen and then stitched me up again. I can feel nothing, just a warm glow. Perhaps I am still high. Close my eyes. Dream of Daisy.

It is morning, and they have come to make me sit up and eat something. There is a menu. 'Just a cup of tea.' The sister is plump and dark-haired; she has a name-tag, 'Ruth', and a small brown mole near the corner of her mouth. Her eyes are a vivid green. 'Temperature, pulse,' she takes the drip out of my hand. 'You're fine,' she says. Outside I can see old women walking slowly around a landing. 'Hip replacements,' says Ruth. 'I have to get them up and make them walk.' Bakewell arrives and tells me I'm OK. 'Everything is Tickety-Boo. We gave you a local anesthetic, you might find it a trifle uncomfortable when it wears off. Nurse will give you some painkillers.'

On the third day, I have started to consider my situation. Daily life has become a ritual. Pills, food, visits from Daisy looking nervous, sleep, read, wash, walk slowly down the corridor to the gents. Occasionally they apply a new dressing. Ruth says, 'Only five more days, then you can go home.' Then she adds, 'Have you been?' and I reply, 'No not yet.' The thought of flexing my stomach muscles is unbearable. My abdomen has become a dull, red pain and I cannot contemplate the possibility of anything that might engage the butchered tissues before they have healed.

I am beginning to worry about my cock and whether Bakewell could have, maybe, suffered a lapse in concentration. I have a vague idea of what goes on down there; of the intricate nest of tubes, nerves and arteries which combine to make everything work. I am beginning to conceive a horror that the old chap has been irreparably damaged and will never work again. I have taken to lifting the sheets and examining it as it lies dormant like some baby's forearm inert across the tapes and bandages on my abdomen.

On the fourth morning, Ruth asks me once again if I have managed to achieve anything serious. 'Perhaps we ought to give you a little encouragement,' she says. 'I'll send a nurse in to give you something later on this morning.' I doze until, at eleven o'clock, there is a gentle knock on the door and I open my eyes and there she is. She is young, black, perhaps nineteen, limpid eyes and a prominent mouth with a hint of pink skin in the soft line where her lips come together. She wears a pale blue gown and a starched white cap, folded like a paper dart. In her hand is a small, enamel, kidney-shaped dish covered by a white cloth. It reminds me of serving mass at school, but I know very well that there are no cruets of wine or water beneath this particular napkin.

She says, 'My name is Deborah, how are you today?' And, as she speaks, she turns slightly and pushes the door shut with her foot. I look at her, avoiding her eyes. She places the dish on the table by my bed, takes a paper pack from the pocket of her gown, opens it and removes a pair of white latex gloves. 'Please turn on your side,' she says softly as she begins to work her long fingers into the tight, smooth, powdered gauntlets. I turn away, listening to the snap of the material on her wrists as she pulls on first one and then the other.

For the first time since the operation, my senses are alert. My skin tingles with a mixture of self-consciousness and anticipation. I want to say something that will break the tension but since she has entered the room, my mind has emptied completely and my heart has begun to hammer in my chest. My hearing seems to be unnaturally acute as I hear her pick up the dish, remove the cloth and pick up the small flexible projectile underneath. I can feel the air on my bottom as she pulls back the sheets. 'Try to move your knees up to your chest,' she says, and, as I bend my legs slowly and painfully, I feel her fingers between my cheeks and I feel the cold of the lubricating jelly on my anus and her finger working its way in and out and then, slowly, she inserts the thing, whatever it is. In a second or two, it is all over and I feel her gently wiping me with the cloth and pulling back the sheets. She says nothing, and, as I turn over and look at her, she casts her eyes at the ground and silently leaves the room.

This morning, Ruth and Dr Bakewell arrive for a chat at nine o'clock. 'Well?' she says, after the surgeon has fiddled around with the dressings and patted me on the head, 'Have we been?' 'Sorry, but it's still no go,' I say, although in truth, Deborah's ministrations had achieved a dramatic and almost immediate effect, news of which I had managed to keep to myself. After my painful sprint down the corridor, I sat in the chair in my room and for the first time since my operation had felt the blood once again stirring in my groin. I thought of Deborah, the student nurse, sent to do the menial jobs. I wondered what had crossed her mind when she came into the room and saw me; all those unspoken thoughts, the sudden, intense intimacy. I imagined how she would have felt if I had been expected to do it to her, the voluntary submission and the inevitable spreading of the cheeks and then the violation of that small, wrinkled orifice, so personal and private.

The thoughts running through my head are almost more than I can bear. I lie in my bed, trying to relax, watching the hands of the clock creep around to eleven, my heart thumping against my ribs. Then I hear the knock and I turn slowly as she slips silently into the room and closes the door. She says nothing, simply walks across to me and puts the dish on the table. I wonder how many others' intimate parts she has invaded this morning. I want mine to be the first. She looks at me and says, 'Sister says you're a naughty boy.' At this I can manage little more than a simpering smirk, as she reaches into her tunic and produces the gloves, crackling in their sterile packaging. 'You know what to do,' she says, stretching and snapping the latex like an elastic band between her hands and slipping the gloves downwards onto her long, brown, elegant fingers.

I do as I am told, turning and folding, my buttocks stretched and vulnerable to her gaze as she pulls back the sheets. And, as inevitably as night follows day, as I feel her cool fingers on my body, my cock begins to swell like a blood-sated vampire and I feel as if there is a vacuum in my chest and my pulse begins to throb and every nerve in my body is on fire beneath my skin. She is rotating her finger slowly around my sphincter and I know in my heart that she is taking longer than before, and at last, as I feel the hard projectile sliding gently between my cheeks, I turn and bring my knees up and clasp her wrist with my left hand, and she is looking at me and I pull her across the bed as I turn and place her white, oily, latex-covered fingers on my cock.

And slowly, she grips it, her thumb along the top and her fingers below, and she starts slowly to move her hand up and down what has now become a live and uncontrollable part of me. The pain has gone, or rather, has been absorbed into the pleasure and I am an instant away from ecstatic oblivion, when the door opens and in comes Sister Ruth.

Not even the fearsome sight of an outraged staff nurse could have begun to restrain my cock which now has a life and will of its own. Desperately, I grip Deborah's hand in mine and keep it where it is, while Ruth stands, petrified, just inside the room. She stares at me for an instant before pushing the door shut, walking slowly across to the other side of the bed and kneeling beside me. Deborah, relaxed now, reaches for the lubricating jelly which she spreads on her gloves before returning to her work. They take it in turns. Ruth leans over and takes me gently in her mouth, while Deborah waits to masturbate me with one hand and play with my sphincter with the other. I lie like a crucified criminal, my hands stretched on either side, beneath the raised tunics of the two nurses, my fingers slippery within their cotton knickers. When I come, it is with a mixture of pain and relief the like of which I have never experienced before or since and as my fluid dances in the air, the girl and the woman kiss, open-mouthed across the bed and I feel the mutual stiffening of the muscles in their thighs.

As she straightens her uniform and pats her hair, sister says my dressings are in a dreadful state and will have to be changed, a task which she completes without a word, wiping my cock with a *Wet One* and leaving me sweet smelling and neatly packaged once again. Deborah says nothing, just smiles and walks away with her dish and a slightly soiled cloth. As Ruth gathers up the dressings, she turns to me and raises her eyebrows. 'No, not yet,' I say, the lie tripping easily off my tongue. 'Well,' she says, 'let's see what happens in the morning. Perhaps we can give you another dose? It's lucky you're a private patient.'

The Honourable Schoolgirl

Lady Isabella Byng stands erect, the yew stave in her hand, bodkinned arrow nocked on to the waxed string and drawn back until the fletching is tight against her cheek. A scrap of silk flutters from the top of the weapon as she releases the arrow and watches it curve gracefully away. Lady Isabella's hair is coiled high on her head and secured with a mother of pearl comb so that it tumbles in dark curls around the collar of her dress. She wears a small velvet hat decorated with satin ribbon and her young body is encased in a long-sleeved, pale blue tunic, tight in the bodice and gathered at the waist with a velvet girdle tied in a bow perched jauntily on the bustle. A leather quiver is slung round her hips and she wears a mitten to protect the fingers of her right hand from the violence of the arrow release. Her little black boots are laced above her ankles but the light breeze plucking at the hem of her dress reveals an occasional glimpse of silken hose. Before her the field stretches towards the cathedral close and the high brick wall which surrounds it. Lady Isabella is not alone, a dozen or so pretty fledglings from Mrs Clifford-Turner's Academy have taken up their positions on either side. The targets stand at a range of fifty yards and the peace of the morning is disturbed only by the distant thud of arrows as they land on the painted canvas and penetrate the soft straw of the butts.

Behind the field, in Symonds Street next to a terrace of ivy-clad red brick Alms houses, stands The Academy, a sombre building, once the home of Dr. Crosbie-Napier, Arch

Deacon at Winchester whose departure for the Bishop's palace ten years ago, coincided with Mrs Clifford-Turner's search for a suitable establishment for the schooling of young women from respectable homes. This sunny, autumn morning, the headmistress stares balefully out of her window and sucks on a black Java cheroot. She wears fashionable tartan with a white silk jabot about her neck, her creamy hair pulled back and tied in a bun. She is aware that Isabella Byng is wilful and into her eighteenth year. Isabella is a tall girl, nearly six feet in height, and although she might be considered plain of feature, her mouth perhaps too generous and her neck a little long, her eyes are wide apart and clear and blue and more than compensate for shortcomings elsewhere. While her gaze is habitually directed down and away from those she addresses, it is when she raises her head and turns her eyes upon the subject of her interest, that she is most captivating. She is the sole issue of an ancient and privileged family whose wealth and estates are legendary. Her schooling has consequently been the subject of much debate amongst those who love her and who have taken great care over her upbringing so that the very idea of an unsuitable liaison creates shudders in the bosoms of her nearest and dearest.

Amusements are not plentiful in the City of Winchester; the clergy who ebb and flow about the Cathedral Close are presently preoccupied with Bishop Napier's slow descent into death after a lingering illness, and whilst there are occasional young masters from the college to keep an eye on, the only worrisome diversions come from the officers stationed at the Cavalry barracks at the Westgate.

Thirty miles to the south-west in the dining room at the Manor House at Upperton which reposes in a thousand acres of its own park, Isabella's mother, Lady Charlotte, has received an alarming letter. It has in fact come from the Headmistress of The Academy and she reads it in the silence of the breakfast table while her husband Lord Markham Byng digests disturbing news from the colonies in *The Times* newspaper which has been ironed and brought to the table by Sambo the coachman. It is nine o'clock and the silence of the room is disturbed only by the distant chiming of a clock in the hall, the rustling of paper and the faint sound of gnashing teeth emanating from his lordship. The news from Winchester is brief and to the point; Lady Isabella has been seen walking in the water meadows with Captain Bradish-Ellames, a subaltern in the Queen's Own Hampshire Dragoon Guards whose regimental Headquarters are in the town. Worse, they have been reported by the Head of House, Milly Curzon, to have been touching, if not actually holding, hands. The incident has been reported to Mrs Clifford-Turner who has seen fit to set pen to paper. The very fact that a letter has been sent is enough to cause alarm. Lady Charlotte decides not to mention it to her husband until she has discussed the matter with the woman. She returns her napkin to its ring and says, 'Charles, I have decided to take the train to Winchester this afternoon. I intend to dine with my sister and spend the night with her.' Immediately after luncheon and accompanied by her maid, Lady Charlotte has herself driven to the station at Sixpenny Handley and one hour later, upon her arrival at the Cathedral City, she summons a phaeton to carry her to Symonds Street.

Mrs Clifford-Turner's room is pleasant enough; comfortable and with a view over the Close. Tea is served from a silver pot and a small Pekingese dog snuffles in its sleep upon the hearth rug. As she takes her seat, Lady Charlotte notices a Malacca cane on the mantle shelf. It has been well used by the look of it and has been embellished with a leather grip. Having quickly established the likely truth of the allegations relating to her daughter's iniquity, she says, 'I cannot impress enough upon you that this business must be put a stop to immediately. You are paid to protect Isabella. She is young and headstrong and I will not have her consorting with anyone outside the school. I want you to deal with the matter and confirm to me that you have done so.' Leaving the cup of tea untouched, she hands the headmistress a card, 'I will be staying in Winchester overnight, you may send a message to this address in the morning. Good day to you.'

After Lady Charlotte's departure, Mrs Clifford-Turner calls Emily Curzon to her room. The girl arrives, an expression of eager anticipation on her face, and is cross examined in every detail until there seems no doubt at all that Isabella has not just broken the rules of the school, she has exposed herself to an unmentionable risk against the expressed wishes of her family. 'What makes you certain that it was Captain Bradish-Ellames walking with her in the water meadows?' asked the headmistress. 'I saw them emerge together from the family's house in the Romsey Road,' said the girl, 'and he was wearing his regimental dress uniform. I cannot imagine who else it might have been.' The headmistress sighs and makes a note in her pocket book. 'Go and find Isabella and bring her to me,' she says, tossing her venerable head and setting her lips in a thin line. 'I want you here while I deal with her.' As the girl bows and leaves on her errand, Mrs Clifford-Turner picks up the Malacca rod and runs it between her fingers, cutting with it sharply through the air and raising it to her lips as if it was a hand to kiss. She smiles and perches a generous haunch on the side of the table while she waits for the evening to burst into life.

Isabella is in her room. She is composing a letter to her lover. 'My body and soul are yours,' she writes, 'I dream of the touch of your hand and your sweet breath on my skin.' After a while she lays down the pen, leans back on to the chaise longue, her eyes closing as she recalls the stillness of the water meadows in the dusk, sees again the brilliant night sky reflected in the mirror of the chalk stream, hears the carol of a moorhen fussing on the river bank. For the first time in her young life, she has learnt to appreciate the power of a pounding heart, how her body liquefies under the touch of a hand on her breast, to understand her desire to give herself to her lover. Unconditionally. She feels once more the damp autumn air on her legs as she raises herself, pulling up her dress as she lies in the meadow grass, aware that her hand has been taken and that it is lost in the stiff folds of a cavalry officer's uniform and she feels the delirium of the touch of hot skin and sinew and the bold reality of hair and scent and of her body opening like a flower. She tries to recall the details of how, suddenly, her mouth has become wet with someone else's saliva, of a tongue like a fish in the pocket of her cheek, of the fear mixed with joy as her loins are infused with heat and the sensation of the viscous, spilling nectar drenching her most intimate place. She experiences once more the vacuum in her throat as she sits alone, smiling, the letter before her, her hand, soft in the folds of her dress.

Emily Curzon gathers herself briefly before the door, raps her knuckles on the wood. 'Lady Byng, come with me please. Mrs Clifford-Turner has asked me to bring you to her immediately.' And so it is that the girl, her dreams spinning like dying embers about her, is brought to the headmistress and made to stand on the rug with her back to the fire. She smiles. 'Isabella, I have asked you to come to me because of a disturbing report relating to your behaviour and because your mother has expressed concern about you and has asked me to deal urgently with the matter. I am after all responsible for your education and consequently for your virtue.' She takes a deep breath, pulls back her shoulders and spits the words, 'You have been seen with a man, worse than a man, a soldier, a Captain Bradish-Ellames in circumstances which can only be described as questionable. There is, however, no question but that you are guilty and I have decided to put an end to this nasty little intrigue once and for all. Because I wish to make an example of you, I intend to thrash you before the whole school. It is how we deal with unacceptable behaviour and there is no reason to make any exception in your case. Have you anything to say before I have the girls called to assembly?'

Isabella, the blood rising to her cheeks, looks around the room. She notices the Pekingese, the smouldering grate, Emily, a self righteous smile on her lips. She glances at the cane, lined up on the desk between a pair of heavy glass ink-wells.

'Madam,' she says, taking a breath and looking into the

eyes of the headmistress, 'sadly, I have never met Captain Bradish-Ellames. Who has told you that I have?' Mrs Clifford-Turner raises a hand and indicates the Head Girl. 'I saw you walking with him through the water meadows at North Walls,' says Emily, 'You touched each other. He was in uniform.'

Isabella, a sudden pallor on her cheeks, leans forward and picks up the cane. 'Madam, Captain Bradish-Ellames has been missing in the Crimea since two months. He is believed killed. It was his sister, Millie you saw me with. In her unhappiness, she has taken to wearing her brother's dress uniform and I have taken it upon myself to comfort her whenever I can.'

The words hang in the air like a cloud of gas until Isabella, who is nothing if not muscular, breaks the tension by bending the Malacca rod until it snaps with a crack like the discharge of a small pistol. 'I will deal with my Mother,' she adds, picking up the card from the headmistress' desk and turning on her heal. 'Good bye.'

And so it was that Lady Isabella Byng and Miss Millicent Bradish-Ellames set up home together and managed to disappoint their relatives for many years. That they were lovers was a subject which was never considered or discussed within the family or by the world at large, and tonight they lie secure in each others arms, almost naked and incandescent in their love, while Isabella, wearing only an unbuttoned cherry coloured mess jacket, which once belonged to a trooper in the Light Brigade, buries her face in the dewy softness of her lover who has facilitated access by slipping her cavalry britches half way down her thighs.

Mathilde leant forward in the director's chair, arching her back while a girl gummed tiny pearls to her eyelashes. Someone was painting her lips with a long brush and a boy held her hair, brushing it down her back until it shone like black enamel. Models ran into the room, tugging at their clothes as they hurried to the mirrored tables where their familiars waited to return them to the catwalk. Mathilde, her nipples dabbed with a cold cloth until they stood like switches, was naked. They worked on her, dropping a concoction of black lace and white satin embroidered with chinoiserie across her shoulders. Then she stood aloof, eyes shut, red and yellow painted nails held away from her body, and thought meltingly of Rudi.

When the man in headphones beckoned, Mathilde unravelled like a snake and stalked across to the dark of the stage where she emerged like an ebony flamingo into the valley of saturated wealth. Faces blurred left and right and batteries of cameras crackled like small arms fire before her. Her legs looped and swung; her feet on their spikes landing meticulously on the piste. She stopped a metre from the drop, glanced scornfully down at the reptiles struggling for angles in the pit, turned on her heel, swung her hips and swayed her glorious buttocks languorously back into the underworld.

Afterwards, Mathilde shrugged into the little gossamer Chanel and pulled on the satin slingbacks. She grabbed her Lynx jacket and a purse and strode through the foyer of the Carlton, past the stone-faced women from PETA and out to the cream Mercedes waiting below the steps.

Later, she sat in the VIP lounge waiting for the flight to Kennedy to slide up on the liquid black screen. Contemptuous of the adoring gaze of ordinary men and women, she avoided any risk of eye contact. She knew that most hearts missed a beat when she passed by. Anyway, Rudi was flying the midnight long haul to New York and Mathilde wanted him to remember the journey for the rest of his life.

~

Beneath her, in the bowels of the terminal, the Economy Class queues stretched across the marble floors like hedges in suburbia. It was September 7th and the exodus from Europe back into the US was in full flow. Groups of men, women and children dressed in black hats and long coats straggled across the marble floor. The Hasidim had reached the second stage of their journey home to Brooklyn and their ringlets drooped like damp tassels across their pale cheeks. The women, weigh-faced and sweating in wool, struggled to control the children.

~

As the 747 touched down at Nice en route from Vienna, Rudi Klein pulled the earphones from his head, handed control to his First Officer and strolled into the crew rest room. He pulled his cock from his uniform and held it in a stream of warm water beneath the aluminium tap, massaging it in almond scented lotion from a plastic bottle. He took a paper towel and wiped the skin. He had spent last night at the Club Mons Veneris in Tata and was uncomfortably aware of the raw patches smarting beneath his foreskin. Rudi changed into a clean shirt, straitened his tie and dabbed a smear of *Infanta* into the hollow of his neck.

Mathilde boarded at 11.50. She turned left and settled down in the single seat at the front of the first class cabin. A stewardess handed her a glass of Moet. She pushed the button, reclined the seat, closed her eyes and dozed.

At 00.15, the great aircraft, finally loaded with noisy, nervous Hasidim, lumbered into the air and banked away to the west above the Corniche and the glittering necklace along the throat of the Cote D'Azur. As they levelled off and relaxed, a stewardess handed Mathilde a dish on which she had placed slices of fresh lemon, a pot of beluga, a silver spoon and a sealed envelope. The note, written on silver card and signed 'R' said, 'Business Class, 02.00'.

Mathilde squirmed, crossed her legs and gripped her thighs together. She loved the anticipation almost more than the act itself. After a moment or so she lifted the hem of her skirt, tucked a finger into her pants, pulled them down over her shoes and slipped them into her purse. She opened her legs a little, felt the tepid breeze from the air conditioning on her skin. She enjoyed exposing herself; anyone standing before her now would see the delicate brown lips of her pussy; she opened her thighs a little further, brought her knees up, placed her index finger on the soft skin at the top of her leg, tugging it gently so that the voluptuous, pink, wet flesh of her vagina was open and exposed. She sighed, gently moving her hips from side to side; bracing and relaxing her pelvic muscles until her heart raced and she began to come. Her contractions lasted for almost a minute while she breathed through her nose, until the end, when she released a gasp of air through her mouth. After a moment she slid an index finger into the slippery furrow of her sex and brought it to her face, breathing in the rich, fetid scent before removing a small Sony digital camera from her bag and holding it between her knees, pointing it towards her and opening her legs a little wider. She pressed the shutter twice and removed the memory stick, sealing it into the envelope and telling the stewardess to return the letter to Captain Klein.

They were serving snacks in Economy where the demand for Kosher food was creating tension amongst the crew. From time to time, the male Hasidim would move into the aisles where they would chant and bob their heads. The sprinkling of Christians in the cabin looked nervously about them and gulped their alcohol, eying the children running in the aisles. The first officer was making his final announcements before dimming the cabin lights. 'We have reached our cruising altitude of 45,000 feet at a ground speed of 560 miles per hour. In a few minutes will cross the Atlantic coast at San Sebastian on our way to New York. We expect to be on the ground at Kennedy at 03.00 hours local time.'

The 747 slipped westward like a city in the skies. Rudi would fly the aeroplane for two hours from take off and take control again for the approach and landing in New York. At 02.00, he handed over control to his First Officer, pulled off his headphones, stretched and walked through the rear of the flight deck and into the Crew Bunk, He shut the door, looked at himself in the mirror above the hand basin, and smiled at his reflection.

At 02.00 hours, Mathilde slipped upstairs into Business class, walked through the dimmed cabin and knocked gently on the partition behind the flight deck. The door opened immediately and she fell forward into her lover's arms.

During the last twenty four hours, they had thought about little but what they were going to do to each other. Mathilde's fevered desire had created a vacuum in her body and an almost painful pounding in her heart. The images lodged on the memory stick had exerted a powerful impact on Rudi's libido and the result was that their mutual urgency dispelled any possibility of finesse. She took a shoe from him, threw it away, ripped at his uniform, cut her fingers on the zip as she tore at the serrated metal. She was above him, back arched like a bitch, her tongue in his ear, his mouth. In a minute, apart from a sock, he was naked below the waist and she gorged on him, took his balls in her hand, his cock into her hot throat, turned and swung her hips above his face, her knee thudding against the bulkhead as she turned. She felt nothing but his mouth in her hot sex while he held her, pulling himself upright behind her, pushing her waist down onto the bed until her buttocks were stretched and spread before him, and, breathless and congested with blood, he could plunge himself into her so that she screamed, out of control, her arms thrashing the sheets, tears streaming down her face, her ecstasy taking her to the edge of consciousness, her orgasm hitting her like an avalanche.

~

They were two and a half hours into the flight when a stewardess dozing in the galley behind the central staircase, realised that something was amiss. Ever since taking off, small groups of Hasidim had been leaping to their feet and chanting from the book of the *Torah*. The Hasidic faith is nothing if not overt and at 02.35 local time, around one hundred and twenty male Jews wearing hats and together weighing a total of ten and a half tons, left their seats and moved towards the rear of the fuselage where they began to chant and pray. The First officer sat up with a start. For no apparent reason the aircraft had started to climb and within seconds the autopilot had tripped out and the flight crew, who had no idea what had caused the change in pitch, had started the recovery process to bring the 385 ton plane back into level flight.

It was as if the aircraft had hit a hump backed bridge. The fuselage creaked and shuddered and passengers strapped into their seats woke up and started to scream. Aircrew refer to it as 'Negative G' and it has the effect of making everything not secured or tied down weightless and rise to the ceiling. The congregation of 125 Hassidim worshiping their God at the rear bulkhead, together with Rudi and Mathilde approaching their second tumultuous climax in the crew bunk, shot miraculously upwards. The Chief Steward's shouted plea to fasten seat belts coincided with the economy cabin filling with flying bodies.

Mathilde, in the throes of her convulsive and passionate spasm, hit the ceiling simultaneously with Rudi and fell, semi-conscious, back onto the rumpled blankets of the bunk. 'Jeeesus Christ,' she screamed while her heart pounded within her ribcage and blood from a cut on the bridge of her nose streamed down her face and into her mouth. Rudi, although stunned, was able to twist open the door and stagger toward the flight deck, pulling up his trousers as he went.

The incident, officially described as a hydraulic malfunction, has never been fully reported. The aeroplane made an emergency landing at Shannon, a few injured passengers were removed and Rudi was grounded prior to an investigation by the Civil Aviation Authorities. Mathilde, meanwhile, overwhelmed by her miraculous escape, travelled on to Brooklyn where, for the first time in her young life, she started to sleep with men whose bodies had never been exposed to the sun. She abandoned Chanel for woollen tights and sensible skirts. After discussions with an old man with a beard, she has changed her name to Judith.

There is little to recommend the republic of Albania to the pursuer of leisure. Ever since the Tupolev smacked down onto the runway at Tirana ten days ago, it has been a series of riots and assaults on the senses. Men in leather jackets fighting in the arrivals hall, the dead horse outside my hotel, bloodstains on the seats of my minder's Mercedes. Progress south along the coast is completed in short, nerve-wracking jerks against a background of the glittering Adriatic. Sergei, who is being paid $100 to drive me, says little, just keeps his eyes on the road, chain smoking and occasionally warning me not to get out of the car.

Now we have at last arrived in Saranda to discover that there isn't a bed to be had. Sergei's brother, Artan, is under interrogation, his house is full of police and the road is blocked. I sit in the car and wait. 'There has been a riot and my brother's 'ooman 'as been shot,' says Sergei, when he comes back an hour later. 'E doan' know why is happen. She is talking on the 'phone when some focker kick in the fron' door and shoot 'er in the arse. Is not good and she 'as goan to 'ospital in Greece because the bullet, 'e is still up there.' He shrugs, 'Artan say to wait for 'im at the Suleiman Bar.'

We drive through the smoking wreckage of the port, past groups of unshaven and sullen men with half-closed eyes, policemen with guns and long night sticks clustering around armoured personnel carriers in the square. At the docks, the rotting hulls of speedboats stolen from the Greeks, their engines stripped out and long ago sold to Italian smugglers, have been bulldozed into piles, a solitary symbol of local enterprise.

Half a mile down the coast, the Suleiman, modern, glass and aluminium, checked table cloths and swarthy waiters, is empty. We take a seat in a window over the sea and order a bottle of raki. 'Who owns this?' I ask. Sergei looks at me and shrugs, 'Wait until Artan come, e'll tell you.' His brother slips through the door at seven o'clock. He runs his hand through his short hair and lights a fag. Nothing is said. Slowly the restaurant begins to fill up. Men come briefly to the table and silently grip his shoulder or ruffle his hair, presumably as a way of showing sympathy for what has happened. No words are exchanged. 'Is because you are here,' says Sergei. 'They doan know you.'

The evening sun, a deep orange yolk sinks into the purple haze over Corfu and harsh lights flicker on in the restaurant. Sergei and Artan are drinking their way steadily through the raki and all the tables but one are full. Big men, hairy bellies poking through tight white shirts, gold medal-lions, Omega watches. Waiters, slovenly and at odds with the cool, grey marble and metal, lounging, bored, against the bar. A Ukrainian girl, blond hair in braids, her long body squeezed into white, bell-bottomed pants and a yellow silk shirt, sits silently, eyes downcast beside a tall, expressionless Turk, liver-coloured freckles on his shaved skull. 'Is Joe,' volunteers Artan. 'E owns the Suleiman, 'e's just out of prison in Athens, 'e done a rape.'

At eight o'clock, Sergei gets unsteadily to his feet and leaves without aword, his cigarette left half-extinguished on a side plate. His brother, still silent and morose, sighs, fiddles with the menu and orders lobsters and bottles of Shesh I Zi wine. While we eat in silence, I can see that the last table has filled. Twelve men and women sitting silently, staring at their plates and there is a girl, her hair tight in a long pigtail hanging down her arched back, her arms bare, a tattoo visible just below her right shoulder. When she catches my eye she looks quickly away.

We finish the meal, and Artan, glancing occasionally at Joe and checking his watch, drinks his way through a second bottle of wine. Of Sergei, there is not sign. The Suleiman, now full, is subdued. I know how much noise is generated by a room full of Albanians and it is considerably more than this. There is a cloud of tension over the town and adrenalin is stiffening my limbs and tightening my stomach.

Sergei finally returns at eleven o'clock with a thin youth in a well-cut black leather jacket. On his T shirt, the death's head of Christ from the Turin shroud. He wears a solitary gold earring and where his other ear should be is a mess of mangled cartilage; his fingers are stained with nicotine, his nails bitten. He takes the seat beside me, 'Barbouche,' he says, 'I am travel agent.'

Artan kisses Barbouche on both cheeks and the more relief I see in his face, the more nervous I become. He turns to me, 'Look, there will be trouble here tonight and you are not safe. Barbouche will take you to Corfu in boat. Is all right, he is expert and do it every night, no problem. Very fast.' 'What the fuck are you talking about?' I ask. 'The Greek navy has gun boats in the channel and I have a ticket for the ferry.' But I know perfectly well that my new travel arrangements for Corfu are already decided and that they will include me, the clothes I stand up in and the dozen illegals sitting at the table across the room. 'Leave your kit with me,' says Artan, 'is OK, you 'ave no problem, you 'ave a passport. No one else has any papers. Barbouche, 'e only charge you $200.'

~⌒~

And so I find myself, at two in the morning, lying in a RIB in a rocky cove on the coast a mile west of Saranda. I have my wallet, passport and a map of Corfu round my neck in a plastic bag and I'm wearing tennis shoes, jeans and a dark blue shirt. My only weapon is half a bottle of Albanian Skandabeu brandy. With me are twelve illegal immigrants and Barbouche who has changed into a wet suit and is carrying a rusty Kalashnikov and hissing orders to make us spread our weight efficiently along the inflatable sides of the boat. There are no life jackets. I can see the dark mass of the island, tantalizingly close across the strait. Occasionally, headlights swing like shooting stars along the coast road above the beach at Agios Spiridon.

Barbouche fires the engines and we are away and out of the cover, immediately drenched in spray and hammering across the waves. 'Ten minutes to cross to Spiridon,' Artan had said, but tonight is different and as we rush at 30 knots towards Corfu, engines screaming as we bounce out of the water, the little boat is suddenly picked out in a brilliant light, etched sharp against the night sky and I can hear a man's voice magnified electronically in the distance and the short burst of gun fire which follows. Barbouche turns, his face ghostly white in the searchlight. His hair blowing straight back, his mutilated ear, exposed, and I see him lift the automatic weapon to his shoulder and fire a wild burst towards the light, screaming 'Special Forces' into the night air and gunning the motors.

The gunfire intensifies and, convinced that I am about to join Artan's girlfriend with a bullet up my arse, I go, rolling over the gunwale, falling sideways into the sea and bouncing about in the swell until I am sucked beneath the black water.

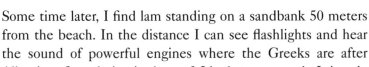

Some time later, I find Iam standing on a sandbank 50 meters from the beach. In the distance I can see flashlights and hear the sound of powerful engines where the Greeks are after Albanians floundering in the surf. I look at my watch. It is only 20 minutes since we left. I must stay in the water until the beach is deserted. Of Barbouche and the RIB there is no sign.

Wading towards the shoreline an hour later, shivering in the battle-grey dawn, I make out the shape of a figure lying on the sand, arms outspread, feet still in the water. Her hair unraveled now, plastered down her back. I turn her over to feel for a pulse in her neck but my hands are so cold. As I hold her she opens her eyes and looks up and I know she is all right and I pull her arm across my shoulder and take her around her waist and half walk, half carry her until we are in the shelter of the dunes where we lie down on the sand, holding each other for warmth. She drifts into unconsciousness, her head heavy on my shoulder.

In the strengthening light, I look at the girl, asleep on her back, her hands clasped between her legs; her eyelids fluttering like moths. Close to, I can see the crystals of sea salt around her mouth, the damp curl of her hair, the once perfect pigtail undone during the violence of her escape. I examine her breasts, rising and falling softly, free beneath her loose shirt, and when she turns on her side, her thin jeans are dry but for a dark, damp patch between her legs, and when she removes her left hand from the warmth of her thighs and slowly places her thumb in her mouth, I am overwhelmed with desire. I remove her canvas shoes and massage her feet, pick up her hand and stretch her fingers between mine, I look into her ears, and, inside the loose folds of her shirt, at her nipples and, as the sun rises to the west above the accursed mountains of Albania and begins to flood our bones with warmth and life, I watch her open her eyes, blink and give me a solemn look. I take her in my arms, as if to protect her, but in truth, in the aftermath of the dangerous night, I want her so badly that my heart is hammering against my ribs and I am radiating heat like a red hot furnace.

'Who are you?' she says, 'And where is this place?' I look around, the beach is deserted. Of the Special Forces boat, there is no sign. The fresh morning sea is lapping on the shingle, gently dragging the line of rattling stones back and forth. In the distance, I can hear bells as a flock of goats wanders though an olive grove up by the road. There is the faint scent of wild rosemary in the air. 'We're in Corfu,' I say. 'Give me a kiss,' and she smiles and reaches for me and pulls me down to her mouth, taking my hair in her fist and laughing as she opens my lips with her tongue. Then we are rolling in the sand, and my hand is on her breast, on the stiff nipple and I can feel her arching herself up and into my belly and I reach down to pull her pants away and over her thighs and my face is in her silken groin and I can taste the rich earthiness of her. And we are stretching and wrestling with our clothes until we are naked and our bodies are dusted with sand and still damp from the sea. 'Come,' she says, reaching into my groin, taking my cock and, with her eyes on mine, begins to clean away the grains of sand with her fingers and then with her tongue until I am in her mouth and down her throat and it is almost more than I can bear. 'You must wash me, too,' she says, and swings her legs over my face so that I can take her salty, sandy, corrugated, russet pussy in my mouth and prepare it slowly with my tongue until it is slippery with her salty essence and her little wrinkled anus is lean and sweet, and she moves forward from me, on all fours and I rise behind her and she reaches back and pulls herself apart and I am inside her, and I am as big and as hard as it is possible for me to be, and she cries out and arches her back and I see the curve of my penis rolling and rising inside her like a piston until it is too much for me and I come and come into the soft, warm Greek air over her sinuous bottom and onto the small of her back.

All morning, we lie naked in the shallow sea, caressing until we are ready for each other once more, but it is never really quite the same again and at midday we walk to the road and flag down a bus to Kassiopi where we go our separate ways.

I never saw her again and I don't even know what her name was, but I'll never forget her and the lesson I had learnt that there's nothing like a night of blind terror to really get you going first thing in the morning.

It's true.

Waiting for the Cumshot

You'll find Ferroles twenty miles to the east of Paris. It's a mingey little village surrounded by bleak prairies and autoroutes along which Europeans circumnavigate the city at unfeasible speed. There's a chateau in Ferroles, long and pink and very pretty at first sight, it sits behind wrought iron fencing and is surrounded by formal gardens. The whole is enhanced with a lake full of ducks and, at the moment, a thin dusting of snow. The electronically controlled gates open only after I have been carefully observed.

Nobody lives here apart from the concierge. The owners long ago surrendered to the heating bills and now let it out as a location for hardcore movies. There have been dozens of films made at Ferroles, mostly under the name of Marc Dorcell. But today, it is the Nasdaq quoted PRIVATE who have rented the elegant old pile. The concierge, M. Thiery Wallons, a toothless fellow of unfathomable ancestry has struck the mother lode and has been cast by Italian film Director Alessandro del Mar for the lead in *MILLIONAIRE*, the mega masturbathon featuring Nazi gold, the high life and intercontinental copulation on an unimaginable scale.

Through the front doors and I am into a world of heavy duty cables, middle-aged men with pony tails and hard-faced Eastern European girls in orange Max Factor. An English chef is tossing a salad in the tiny kitchen while a German Shepherd guard-dog sleeps on a gold and purple regency sofa. There is a large portrait of Joseph Goebbels propped on an XIIIth century commode. The rooms seem very cramped and dark.

You don't walk through the front door into a brilliantly lit salon at Ferroles. There are disturbing traces of the seventies in the servants quarters where the lavatory has been decorated in an alarming shade of mauve.

I'm OK, there are journalists everywhere including a German television crew with a young and enticingly self conscious female presenter. Small Dutchmen smoke weed and scribble. I sit in the kitchen with a coffee in a polystyrene cup and hope for an erection.

At 13 hundred hours, a door bursts open and the Director's wife, wearing the grey and black uniform of an SS Obersturbanfuhrer scuttles in. 'Ees cumshot,' she shouts. 'Ee's OK, Ees cumshot. Coming now.' There is tension in the air, my trousers are full of static electricity and there's an unseemly rush from the scullery and into a small salon to the right of the vestibule. Through the door and we find ourselves in the presence of director Alessandro del Mar, who sits in a folding chair and examines his nails while he waits for the 4th estate to settle down.

We find ourselves in a small, gilded room with a badly recovered chaise longue in the centre. Lights and silver painted polystyrene reflectors illuminate the scene, On her back with her legs akimbo is Italian mega star Silvia Lancome and kneeling beside her, working away diligently at his cock, is Max Cortez. Max's cock has seen a lot of action since *le petit dejeuner* and has metamorphosed into an interesting shade of mauve. Alessandro del Mar says, 'Please, ladies and gentlemen, no more flash pictures, we going for cumshot now.' Silence, apart from the faint thrumming noise coming from the chaise longue. 'OK Max, let's go. When I say "now", I want precision jism, right between her tits.' Max, in a floral silk beach shirt is on the short strokes when Alessandro says, 'OK, Silvia, take him by the balls and Max, put your left hand on her thigh.' Max somehow keeps going and I wonder what is flashing through his mind. The notes say he worked in a sex shop in Barcelona until someone told him he should become a porn star. The cameraman is getting closer and in the breathless hush, an unspoken signal passes between director and actor and suddenly there it is, a small, viscous outpouring, expertly directed into the soft valley between Silvia's Alpine breasts while Max emits the appropriate ecstatic expletives.

An hour later, showered and ready to go, I notice that Max Cortez is hovering outside the kitchen and waiting to be paid. 'He has spent all morning coming, and now he is going,' remarks Alessandro philosophically. When the film is released, Max's brief ejaculation will be just another cumshot, over in a few seconds. But I know better. I saw him doing it to order in front of a roomful of the world's media. It was, at the very least, an act of great heroism. What the Spanish refer to as *cojones*.

Fleming sat at the kitchen table, a tin of polish and his Sam Brown before him. It was a scene being simultaneously enacted in homes all over England, he thought; men getting ready to go to war. He lit a cigarette and glanced at Mona as she lifted an iron from the range, tested it with her finger and bent to press a shirt. They had met three months ago and he had proposed within two weeks. They had come home to Buckinghamshire to marry in the little church in Penn and tomorrow he would take the train to join his regiment. In a month he would be on the other side of the world.

The glow of the kitchen fire illuminated his bride, catching the gold in her hair, the body beneath the angular cotton frock. Fleming put down the belt and rose to his feet, slipping an arm around her waist and turning her towards him. She smiled, and raised her mouth and when he picked her up and sat her on the table, he could see their shadows flickering on the walls, see her pull her shoulders back as she drew her skirt to her waist, parted her thighs, pulled him towards her. He felt her soft skin as he fumbled at the dress, lifting it over her head while she slipped the belt from his hips and wrapped her legs around him. For the last time for many years, they became oblivious to the world outside, to the wailing siren on the church roof, the distant drone of aircraft passing overhead. Fleming became light headed, felt that his breath had been sucked from his body. He was unaware even that he had entered her, felt simply that she was part of him, that her willing body was for him his source of power.

He pushed her back, his hands on her breasts and his tongue in the coil of her ear and her mouth was open, her lips engorged and she cried out as she came and he watched her spasm in the firelight and as he stared into her flickering eyes and cascaded inside her, he did not even hear the stick of bombs detonating along the valley half a mile away.

～

At the moment when Fleming threw back his head and roared his love, the creamy Singapore moon was bathing the compound in Changi, illuminating the pale face of Kim Wu kneeling at the window of her cell. It was ten years since Sergeant Parker of the Yorkshire Light Infantry, had delivered her from the desiccated evangelism of the Holy Sepulchre orphanage and sent her to his sister in Penang. Entranced by Kim's innocence and grace, he had posted money every month for her education and had been unambiguously proud when, aged twenty, she taken a job as teacher of English at St Bede's College in Singapore.

But now she had broken the rules. In a dismissive judgment after a complaint from the Governor's wife, the District Magistrate had ruled that Algernon Swinburne was, without doubt, a pervert and defiler of young lives. He had sentenced Kim to a month in prison and twelve strokes of the cane for reading the poem *Dolores* to her class.

'You have corrupted children in your care by instructing them in the evils of self abuse,' he thundered and so she stood, three days later, her heart in her mouth, listening to the thunder of distant guns and waiting for the dawn. The girls in the cell had described what she might expect when the sentence was carried out and she was unsure what frightened her more, the forthcoming impact of the Malacca rod on her buttocks or the knowledge that the Japanese were at the gateway to the citadel.

Sleepless and alert to the sounds of the prison, she began to hear noises, which she could not interpret. A muffled percussion, the sound of a chair being pushed sharply back, the faint clang of steel on stone. She was looking across to the cell door at the moment when it burst violently inwards revealing a jumbled vision of bleeding bodies on the floor and Parker her father, half-naked, wild-eyed, his face and body black with charcoal, a carbine in one hand and a bloody kukri in the other.

The shock of his appearance drained the blood from her face. 'We're going,' he said, and she ran with him out of the tumultuous prison and into the night where the city writhed in its death agony.

Kim saw the tracer arching through the moonlight and heard the crump of shells landing on the Empire docks and as they slipped away through the teeming streets, Parker told her that an Australian brigade had deserted and General Percival was planning to surrender,

'It's anarchy, sweetheart, no place for us, stick close by me,' and by five o'clock they had found their way to Keppel harbour where Parker bludgeoned his way on board a yacht and they set sail to the west and up the Malacca Strait.

For twelve months the old soldier and his daughter worked their way along the Malay peninsula, gathering stragglers as they went, until in February 1943, they crossed the border into Burma and settled in a deserted village in dense jungle east of Moulmein.

~

Parker's arrival preceded by three months the disastrous airborne mission of Captain Euan Fleming of the Burmah Rifles. Fleming, parachuted in at night with his unit from an RAF Lysander, lost his men and most of his equipment during a skirmish with an enemy patrol 50 miles to the east of the Sittang River. He had been in the jungle for three weeks, when footsore, dejected and lost, he emerged onto a hillside 100 yards below a Japanese anti-aircraft battery.

He lay throughout the day, watching the gun emplacement from a shallow gully on the edge of the trees and was beginning to wonder if his legs had become rooted into the earth. His eyes stung, and his shorts were shredded and rotting at the crotch. A shoulder wound, the result of a sword thrust by a Japanese officer who he had subsequently killed, was going bad.

His assets were: a Smith & Wesson service revolver and 21 rounds of ammunition, four Mills grenades, a machete, one garrotting wire, five tins of iron rations, a Royal Air Force compass, four condoms, a copy of *Winnie the Pooh* and a picture of Mona, his wife. But his most potent resource was his fury.

During the morning he had watched the Mitsubishi bomber droning overhead, dropping its flailing human cargo into the jungle 500 feet below. He knew that the plummeting figures were prisoners of war because, in his wanderings, he had come across the rotting corpse of a squaddy hanging from the branches of a frangipani tree. The man's neck had been broken in the fall. His arms were bound behind his back.

Fleming eyed the path above him. His senses, tuned to pick up warning signals told him that something had disturbed the equilibrium; a sound or a shadow somewhere had registered in his mind. He knew that he was being watched and it was not the Japanese officer on the path above him. Fleming reckoned that the Jap was no more than 100 feet away. He could hear his boots on the soft earth, see the bandy legs, the pith helmet, the jodhpurs and the sword hanging from his belt. He could smell the smoke from the man's cigarette and sense his complacency. The bile rose in his throat as the man strolled up and down, sucking at his fag, his round glasses glinting in the sun.

He knew that if he was to inflict serious damage he had to act before his body let him down. Do it tonight, use his grenades and kill as many of the bastards as he could before they got to him, and then he would kill himself. But, as the sun dipped beyond the distant river and he pushed himself out of the gully, a hand was clamped across his mouth and a bony knee forced into his back, pinning him to the earth. A voice whispered in his ear, 'Ayup son, tak it easy, I'm with thee, just do as thy's foockin told.'

He felt himself being dragged through thick undergrowth until he was turned upright and saw two men, mahogany-skinned and thin as whippets, crouching before him in the dusk. Others appeared out of the gloom as Fleming swayed, trying to regain his balance. When he tried to speak, they held him again and whispered in his ear to be quiet. A machete was put in his hand and the party set off fast into the heavy, wet bamboo forest.

In the hours that followed, he waded through rivers and

paddy fields and climbed endless hills. His breath rasping in his throat and his shoulder throbbing like a drum, until he abandoned all sense of time, and lost consciousness.

Fleming opened his eyes. He lay naked on a bed fashioned from bamboo in a hut built of thatch with matting walls. His wound had been dressed and the grime and blood washed from his body. His weapons were laid on a mat by the bed. A girl stood by the open doorway, and as he caught her eye, she brought her hands together and smiled, watching him over her steepled fingers. She wore a *longyi* and a bodice of green silk, her feet were bare, her black hair swept back, her eyes prominent above high cheekbones. As he laboriously swung his legs over the edge of the bed, she turned and slipped away.

Within five minutes of his waking, six men had joined him in the hut. One said, 'I'll not introduce myself other than to say that you can call me Parker. We said goodbye to the Army in Singapore and we've been watching you and we'll help you deal with yon gun. Afterwards, you'll likely never see us again.'

Fleming looked up, saw the cropped head, military moustache, tendons racked like hickory in the neck, the cold eye. He glanced at the others. These were hard fighting men. He turned his head. 'I don't deal with deserters,' he said. There was no discussion and by the time he looked up, he was alone. He lay down and was asleep again almost immediately.

As he slept, Kim Wu stood in the doorway watching him as he lay naked on the thin mattress. He slept with his thumb in his mouth, his slim white body patterned with mahogany where his skin had been exposed to the sun. He was no more than a boy, she thought. She looked at his skinny flanks and his blistered feet and wondered how long he had been wandering in the forest.

She arranged food on the floor; rice and fish in a wooden bowl, a plump coconut full of milk. As she straightened, she saw his cock, just a few inches away; fresh as a bamboo shoot, she thought, draped innocently on top of his thigh. She wondered how many months it had been since a woman had arranged her lips around that springy little muscle. As she passed her mouth above his face, felt his breath on her cheek, he sighed and turned over, straightened a knee and slipped an arm between his legs. She studied his bottom; pale and muscular. She saw the soft down at the base of his spine and the dimples at his hips. Her face an inch away from his waist, she examined his skin, the angle of his hip, the little wound of his navel. His eyelashes were like a girl's, she thought, black and curled; his torso, almost hairless but muscular and firm, even in repose; just the scarlet blemish of the wound on his shoulder. She examined his nipples until she was so close to him that she could feel her breath reflected back from his skin. There came the familiar lurch in the pit of her stomach, the blood rising in her neck. She shifted so that she could, if she wanted, take his cock in her mouth. She inhaled, a faint musk, and she felt an overpowering desire to have him. She lay beside him and nuzzled the hollow between his neck and his collarbone.

Fleming returned to instant consciousness with no idea where he was. For days he had slept on the earth and as he lurched to his left, instinctively reaching for his pistol, he fell from the low bed onto the bowl of rice and fish. He stared wild-eyed at the smiling girl on his bed, her lips apart as she reached behind her to unbutton the silk bodice. Fleming stood up, coughed and started to scrape the food from his buttocks. He was aware of her saliva drying on his skin, could still feel her tongue working its way around his throat. He looked at her little brown breasts, sinuous as snakes, the curve of her bottom as she unwound the *Longyi* and when she reached for him, smiling into his eyes and taking his cock in her fingers. pulling him towards the bed. He could not resist, and she stood up before him and he could feel her brown body against his and he was lost. She slipped close behind him, her thighs against his, nuzzling his neck, her hands around his waist, taking his prick and holding it in a soft, mobile grip, moving her quick fingers until he felt a desperation and a dryness in his mouth.

Once again the world around him ceased to exist. He could not hear the scream of parakeets or smell the food roasting on a fire outside. He lay with the girl beneath him, her legs stretched apart and he could feel her slippery thighs and his cock was inside her, his hands on her breasts, and she was offering herself up to him and when, all too soon, his body caught fire and he came with a molten rush inside her. She stared into his faraway eyes and reached up her arm to hold him.

Throughout the day they lay together in the cool of the hut, while she told him about Singapore and the man she had learned to call her father and their odyssey up the peninsular. In the late afternoon as the sun dipped behind the trees, the men came to take the now compliant Fleming back into the bamboo. They moved fast through the endless tangle of vines and tropical vegetation and he had no idea where they were until, at midnight, they emerged onto the slope below the battery.

They rested until the early hours, watching and waiting, and the morning sun was a dim glow behind the trees when they slipped up the hillside to garrotte the sentries and cut the throat of the radio operator. They took the huts together, rolling grenades through the windows and using their kukris on anyone who came out. It was all over in fifteen minutes and while Parker and his men looted the guard house, Fleming adjusted the elevation of the gun and primed and set the timers in the magazine. And as the sun rose above the distant rivet, he lit a cigarette and sat in the gunner's chair and waited, listening for the distant drone of the Mitsubishi on its morning sortie.

TORNADO

For what it's worth, I have my own by-line, Reporter: Valerie Kirk. I work for Collum Macbeth, a white-haired, short-arsed Scottish hack with a red-top intellect and eyes which never stay still. He likes to see his female reporters getting their hands dirty and struts about the back bench with his cronies, going out of his way to treat us like recalcitrant schoolgirls. But I have his measure and when the heat's off in the pub, I treat him like a pile of poo.

This morning, he appeared by my desk where I was idly searching for SM and Restraint websites on the Dog Pile search engine. 'Valerie,' he said, 'there's been a nasty accident in East Anglia. An RAF Tornado has crashed, killing the pilot and navigator. I want you to go up to Coningsby and take a flight in one. It's all arranged with the MOD and I want an overnighter for Thursday. Pull it to bits.' He passed me a number to call and walked away, looking smug.

I am not scared of flying, although I have never flown in a military jet and I know nothing about Tornadoes. The cuttings painted a picture of a battle-scarred old kite which had been modified to carry new weapons systems and is very fast. It was delivered to the RAF in 1984, however, and isn't really sophisticated enough for modern aerial warfare. Ten years ago when Max Hastings took a flight in a Tornado, *Private Eye* described his experience as 'stressful'. The crews had taken exception to Hastings's opinion of RAF performance in the Falklands war and the pilot had ensured that the great man regurgitated his lunch into his oxygen mask a few seconds after take-off.

~

I caught a train to Lincoln in the afternoon, arriving at Coningsby three hours later. It is a vast, grey military stockade in the middle of the fens. The buildings are camouflaged with wavy shapes of green and black and lethal aircraft lurk in anti-blast hangars scattered around the base. The Station Commander, Air Commodore Packer, is a short, neat man with a thick neck and bits of braid and blue stripes all over his flying suit. He was nervous, worried perhaps that he was going to end up in the *News of the World*. 'Have you ever flown in a fighter aircraft before?' he asked. 'We'll have to give you a medical and a bit of a briefing in the ejection simulator. Then you'll need to have your helmet fitted. You'll be flying with Wing Commander Caxton in the morning. You'll be in good hands.'

After a few minutes, to his obvious relief, I was called for by the medical orderly who decanted some pee, checked my blood pressure and sent me off for my helmet and mask. 'We'll do the rest in the morning,' said the orderly, 'have you sorted out with G-trousers and a flying suit. I should get a good night's sleep if I were you.'

My berth for the night, the officers' mess, was a silent and gloomy red-brick building with large, public rooms inhabited by solitary men in unfashionable armchairs reading *The Sun*. My bedroom was sufficiently drab to ensure that I dropped off to sleep at nine and woke up fresh and rested at seven the next morning. After breakfast, I was made to sit in a dummy ejection seat and watch a video film of what to do in an emergency. You reach between your legs where you will find a yellow and black loop, which you pull. This activates the ejector system, shattering the canopy above your head and igniting the rocket beneath your seat. 'Very exciting,' said the instructor, 'like sitting on an Exocet.'

I was wearing a grey, woolen sweater above a pair of admittedly tight, black House of Harlot leather pants and a pair of cowboy boots with stiletto heels when I arrived for my fitting. Beneath my pants I was sporting a pair of tights and no knickers. I never wear knickers unless I have to. What's the point? A tall, camp-looking man carrying a helmet and a life jacket was waiting for me. 'Hi,' he said, 'I'm Tom Caxton, you'll be flying with me.'

Caxton had perfect hair, flawless skin, clear eyes and was wearing a crisp, newly laundered flying suit. He smelt faintly of *Aramis*. 'Tosser,' I thought. Two uniformed men stood behind the counter. 'We will fit your flying suit,' said one, picking up a clipboard and turning to look at my breasts. 'Yes and some G-trousers,' said the other, a bullet-headed NCO with a sergeant's stripes on his bicep. 'Gina will sort you out.'

The Squadron changing room was festooned with khaki garments hanging like tobacco leaves above lines of square lockers, each containing a pair of leather flying boots. Gina was black and impassive, her silence enhanced by a smile and a cocked eyebrow. She was holding a pair of khaki overalls, folded down so that I could climb into them. I stepped out of my pants and felt her eyes on my behind.

'The flying suit zips up the front from the crotch to the neck and should be snug around the hips,' she said. Well it was certainly snug around mine; I could feel it tucked into my pussy, the seam running up the back between the cheeks of my bottom and making me conscious that I was in a military base staffed by 2,000 men whose eyes would be drawn to my buttocks. And this was not the world-weary newsroom of a newspaper, this was no-nonsense country.

Gina said, 'Now for your G-trousers,' and, looking at me with arch appraisal, she selected a pair from a line of stringy, shapeless garments. 'Pull them up over your flying suit and zip them tight at the hips,' she said. At the side of the trousers is a short tube fitted with a valve which clips into the hydraulic system in the cockpit. The legs are open on the inside and have to be laced up by hand. Gina said, 'When you pull G, your trousers inflate, forcing the blood back into the top half of your body and making sure you don't black out.'

Gina knelt behind me to lace up the legs and I could feel her hands on the inside of my thighs as she fiddled with the cords. For a while I could sense her finger resting in my crotch, along the seam where the lips of my pussy were pulled apart by the tightness of my flying suit. It was as if she was touching a wound, and I felt myself beginning to respond. I moved a fraction backwards and her hand remained, maintaining its pressure. I began to sense the juice forming inside me, lubricating the lips of my vulva. When this happens, I emit a scent which infuses everything around it, and which drives me crazy.

I turned to avoid her hand resting on my perineum and found that by facing the other way, her mouth momentarily rested on the thin layer of fabric separating my bush from her face. She sat back on her heels, licked her lips and said, 'Now let's just fit you with a life jacket and some boots and that's you done.'

Forty minutes later, after a briefing in the Ops room, I walked out to the aircraft with Caxton. I was carrying nearly two stone of equipment on my body and I found it difficult to walk. The aircraft was standing in a small hangar, the wings drooping and the fuselage bulging round the two massive engines. I climbed up the ladder and stepped into the rear cockpit, lowering myself into the tiny space. Caxton leaned over me and clipped the oxygen mask across my mouth and nose. Then he began to strap me in, pulling the webbing harnesses tight across my shoulders and between my thighs and clipping them together in a fat metal buckle. He threaded the leg restraints through the garters on my shins and clipped the hose on my G-suit into the bracket on the side of the cockpit.

The restraining tightness of the harness and the flying clothes and the weight of the helmet made me feel that I was trapped in a metal hutch. I was tied in as securely as a condemned woman on the electric chair. Never in my life had I been so helpless, so out of control; never had I felt so aroused. Before me was an unknown length of time when I would be in the power of a man I did not know and, frankly, did not like the look of. With great difficulty I moved my hips forward until the webbing of the harness was tight against my pussy, then I started to move myself from side to side. Caxton lowered himself into the pilot's seat, pulled the canopy over our heads, switched on the radio and ran through the pre-flight checks.

I have only a vague recollection of the next few minutes. We had taxied to the runway and I heard the tower giving clearance to take off. The aircraft stood vibrating for a while. I remember the stick with its buttons and neat little trigger moving sharply towards me and pressing into my groin; I recall my head snapping back as we left the runway; and I saw above me the zigzag of explosive in the canopy which would detonate if I ejected.

I was being forced backwards into the seat, my head jammed into the headrest and my arms so heavy that I could not move my hands. And the trousers; the trousers had become so tight that I felt as if my legs had been squeezed into a metal tube. And then the sudden release as we came out of the climb and leveled out.

My memories of the flight are of the Tornado soaring in the clouds and skimming at the speed of sound above the grey waves of the North Sea, of the wonderful, painful pressure as we turned sharply to the right at 1,000 miles an hour and my body became five times its normal weight. I remember watching distant aircraft like little silver fish nibbling at the fuel lines trailing from a Hercules tanker; but, most of all, I remember the heat in my loins and the pounding in my temple as I wallowed in my own helplessness, yearning for release.

From time to time Caxton would utter fatuous remarks into my headphones: 'If you feel sick, just look at the horizon,' or 'I'm just about to fly upside down for a minute or so.' But I was too preoccupied with my thoughts to care about responding.

It must have been about twenty minutes after take-off when the idea came to me. Caxton had asked in a teasing voice, 'Now Valerie, how would you like to take the controls for a few minutes?' I ignored him. We were flying level at around 5,000 feet along the north Norfolk coast and, when I turned my head, I could see Brancaster Sands glittering in the winter sunshine away to the left.

'Are you alright, Valerie?' said Caxton, the words tinny in my headphones. The truth is that I had never felt so tense in my life, my body infused with the painful pleasure which comes from extreme restraint. The ecstatic prospect of release was all I could think of and Caxton's offer to hand over control was too good to ignore. I reached forward, pulling away from the headrest and curling my hand round the black and yellow cord. 'Thanks for the flight,' I said. 'I'm off. Have a nice day.' And I pulled it. Bang.

WOW.

MOLLY

olly is twenty one, full of beans and a little crazy after a Chelsea winter. She's down in the country at Daddy's house at Faccombe, heart aflutter, skin tingling in the early spring. Yesterday, in the garden room at Queens, she listened, electrified to Dorian Wellbeloved singing from *Winterreise* and *Lohengrin* with Orphean intensity. The huge man and his resonant diaphragm took her breath away and the sadness of *Der Leiermann* caused her to sob loudly during the interval. Tonight, because she managed to recover her composure and work her magic, Dorian is planning to take the train down into the Berkshire countryside where he's hoping to warble to a different tune.

But now Molly is naked and warm in her bed. Crisp, white cotton sheets and the day ahead to dream about. She loves yellow and the scent of citron. She bathes, wallowing in creamy lime and mandarin, her eyes closed in the scented steam. Afterwards, she looks at her body in the bathroom mirror, runs a hand through her tumbling red hair, revolves slowly, glancing over her shoulder at the valley of her lower back, her tanned, lightly muscled thighs, her perfect bottom. There is an ancient cotton Chesterfield beneath the window of the sunlit chamber, it has faded with age to pale blue, and is as big as a bed, and there she sprawls on fluffy towels and anoints her body with oil, rinsing the valley of her breasts with a light cologne, lounging for a while in the big warm womb. She studies the cavities of her body, runs her long fingers through her pubic hair, applies a light oil, tricks out the curly crown of her titian pudendum, separates the lips of her vulva, takes her muscular little clitoris between her finger and thumb, feels the juices start to run.

Today she will spend more time on herself than usual. At eleven thirty after an early breakfast she dresses in a sleeveless riding shirt with silk under-breeches beneath dark blue endurance jodhpurs, pulls on tall, soft Arat boots, tugs them up to her knees and elbows herself into a tight-waisted Newbury jacket. She plucks a whip from the leather tub in the hall and strolls through the garden to the loose boxes where Annette, her groom has saddled Hector with an Equiflex all tricked out with silver and heavy Arabian stirrups which Daddy brought home from Kentucky. Molly hacks out below the hanger and gallops hard up the ridge to the old gibbet on the crest of the downs high above the little village at Coombe. The saddle is a low-backed leather throne rising in the front to the stubby pommel which sticks up like a handle between her thighs and presses into her groin as she leans forward in the gallop. Hector has been retired to domestic duties after six years in the National Hunt and he moves like a warhorse, broad-backed and full of purpose. As they turn for home, the rhythm of his stride becomes synchronised with the swing of her bones and muscles. The tight embrace of her riding clothes and the creaking heavy saddle bucking beneath her creates a lascivious oscillation within the sinews of her groin.

Snape calls for her in the Mercedes at three. He is slim but with broad shoulders and wears impenetrable black wraparound glasses. There is a small automatic weapon on the seat beside him, a penalty of Daddy's inestimable wealth. Molly throws her crop onto the seat, slides across the leather upholstery and stares unseeingly out of the darkened windows as they slip through a landscape of military neat hedgerows and meadows, some acid yellow with rape and others mock-rustic with well-bred cattle. Down the edge of the Hampshire Downs and through the Woodhays and turning between crumbling columns into a long drive leading between shivering poplars up to Walmsley Manor. Thirty or so graves marked with black metal Celtic crosses hidden in a paddock behind the building are a solitary reminder that this was once a Benedictine seminary, but Molly will never have to wander through this unfortunate memorial, because Bishop Walmsley's ancient residence has been bought by an Arab who has turned it into a spa. She is taken from her car and escorted down stone steps into the cellars where once the monks stored their wine and the jewelled vestments in which they chanted of the glory of God. Molly steps out of her clothes and sinks into a deep, black slate bath, feeling the power of the water jets against her back and, as she slips languorously about, braces herself against the hot currents thundering against the muscles of her thighs and between the cheeks of her bottom, skimming the sweat from her skin and tossing her around the pool like a fish beneath a waterfall.

Govindra in a white silk sari, hair pulled back tight into a bun slips into the dark room, places her hands together and bows, 'Cleansing, cleansing,' she says briskly as Molly emerges, naked from the pool and arranges herself in a soft chair while Govindra bathes her feet in a silver bowl filled with smooth pebbles, oil and lotus blossom. Molly takes silk cloths dipped in orange and palma-rosae from a glass bowl and passes them across her face. After a while Govindra makes her stand and squats in front of her, coating her skin with a paste of honey and ground coral. Scooping the mixture from a sandalwood box, she works the gritty exfoliant into the girl's breasts and belly, pushing her legs apart, works on the inside of her thighs and her groin, separates her buttocks, applying the paste around her wrinkled little anus, then tilting her shoulders forward, fingering the paste around the lips of her pussy. She takes a phial of oils and cream and with her fingers, massages Molly's face and neck, then standing and slipping out of her sari, wraps her arms about the girl, moving against her until, breathless and inflamed, blood pounding in her loins, her own hand in there turning quickly, Molly arches her spine and throws her head back in a climax which comes in a burst of short gasps.

Govindra, her body sticky with honey and ripe with her own juice, takes the girl by the hand and leads her to a shower where she washes her, using her fingers and the drumming jet of water to rinse the dripping, gritty honey out of the crevice of the girls body. 'Come with me,' she says, wrapping her in a robe and removing the moisture from her tingling skin. The treatment room is stark, sandalwood walls, a couch covered in towels with an elliptical headrest, a small, pillow in the centre to ensure that the girl's haunches will be raised. A wooden pail filled with hot, round pebbles steams in the corner. She lies on her back, legs slightly apart as Govindra takes oil and hot, smooth basalt stones in the palm of her hands and starts to work on her arms and feet and the muscles of her legs. It feels to Molly as if the warmth is radiating from the woman's palms, penetrating deep into her body, and she becomes consumed by heat and the stones which, as they cool, are placed on her Shakra points, on her sternum, solar plexus and finally on her forehead. As Govindra moves around her, kneading and probing, the girl loses consciousness and descends into oblivion.

Tucked away in the grounds Snape sits in the armoured Mercedes trying to concentrate on his copy of *Soldier of Fortune*. He thinks of the girl and how he has become aware of her since she has returned from London. He remembers her as a schoolgirl, driving her to Godolphin on Sunday evenings where she would board for a week before coming home on Friday night. Plain little thing. But now she was someone to be taken seriously and her father has instructed him to protect her. It is six o'clock when the mobile on the dashboard buzzes and he eases the car into gear and drives to the front of the building. Molly, changed into a short flowery cotton dress and looking like a little girl once again, stands alone on the steps and Snape is aware of a dangerous ripeness about her, an unnatural, seasoned maturity which makes him nervous. He opens the rear door, watches the curve of her buttocks as she bends and sits, waiting for him to pass her the case packed with discarded riding clothes.

They drive slowly towards Faccombe, down the lanes into the village of Inkpen and through the gathering dusk into the dark face of the Downs, up towards the gibbet, standing like a crucifix on the crest of the hill. He glances in the driving mirror, sees that the girl's knees are apart, that her hands are in her lap and that she is staring at the back of his head. He catches her eye as she leans forward; she says, 'Will you stop here please, I need to pee.' Snape, who has learnt his trade in Angola and Belfast, a man whose career depends on awareness, immediately appreciates his difficulty. He pulls the Mercedes across to the roadside and dims the headlights, nervously alert, watching Molly open the door, step from the back, make her way slowly to the front of car, pulling up her dress and squatting in the pool of light, pants around her ankles, looking up, bracing her stomach, starting to urinate onto the road, defiantly staring at the blackness of the windscreen.

Snape is not a man who encourages the young to take liberties and he knows that the decision he is about to make will probably have a bearing on his future. He leans back, and picks up the crop, turns off the headlights and lithe as a snake, walks to the girl, takes her by her arm and throws her over the bonnet of the car. Snape's ability to incapacitate an adversary is legendary and she finds herself unable to move, her buttocks upwards in the fresh air, flinching from the first cut as Snape brings the crop down hard across her thighs and continues carrying out the punishment slowly and deliberately. She hears the whistle of the whip through the air, feels the pain as it cuts into the muscles of her buttocks, the crack of the soft loop of leather as it hits the bonnet. She is aware of the air being forced from her lungs as she fights the urge to cry out with the pain, kicking hopelessly, tears streaming down her cheeks, defeated on the hot, black metal.

～

As Molly squirms, Dorian Wellbeloved alights at Kintbury, stepping down from the five fifteen Paddington to Great Bedwyn. Although it is cool and he is not perspiring, he removes a silk handkerchief from his breast pocket and dabs vaguely at his brow. There is a Tyrolean look about him tonight with his tweed knickerbockers and green felt hat perched on a large head crowned in thick, curly hair. He notices that of Molly there is no sign. He stands sideways on to the end of the platform, his feet at right angles to each other, his broad chest inflated, his chin up, a solitary figure, alone on the tarmac piste. After a while, he glances across the spiked railings towards the Fox and Hounds adjacent to the car park, picks up his brown Gladstone in which he has packed silk pyjamas, toiletries and a Teddy, and repairs to the saloon bar where he orders a Martini whilst positioning himself in the corner by the till where he can be viewed unobstructed from all angles of the bar.

While Dorian is waiting, Molly looks at her swollen buttocks reflected in the mirror. She understands that the rules have been laid down and she has been told where she stands. The house is empty and silent, and from the bathroom window she can see Snape in his heavy tweeds stalking across the lawn. She watches him stop, light a cigarette, take off his jacket, sling it across his shoulders. She inhales, shutting her eyes, placing a hand between her legs, slipping an index finger into her vulva, studying his broad back, turning to look in the steamy window, smiling, closing her eyes........... Coming.

THE HATCHET

I don't know what made me break the journey home. The need to sit in a pub with a glass of beer hit me somewhere on Salisbury Plain. It wasn't just that I had a thirst like the living death, it was an urge to return to my childhood. I wanted to find that hidden valley where I had kissed a publican's daughter and wasted away four days with her during a blistering Indian summer 40 years ago.

~

I was sixteen when my parents loaded up the Humber and we drove down to the Chutes, a bucolic Shangri La hidden away in the Hampshire countryside. They were planning to spend the weekend carousing at some summer house party, while I was given a room in the pub and told to turn up in clean shirt and Oxford bags at the big house for Sunday lunch.

It was harvest time and the girl knocked on my door in the early morning to bring me a cup of tea. She wore a short cotton dress and her legs and feet were bare, and as she opened the window I could see the outline of her slim body in the morning sunlight. At a loose end, I spent the day wandering around the lanes, watching the harvest and sniffing the rich scent of cut grass. In the late afternoon she had come across me dozing on a pile of bales in the corner of a field and had poured me a glass of cool beer from an earthenware jug. We had walked home together behind a cart piled high with hay and when, after a while, without a word, I put my arm around her waist, we had wandered away as the farm hands rode home before us beneath a night sky full of shooting stars.

She sat on a five-bar gate on the edge of a wood and I buried my head in her lap and she dropped down, sliding her body down my chest, her hands entwined in my hair and her legs around my waist. And when she kissed my dry, unseasoned mouth I saw that she had undone the buttons on her cotton dress and I could feel her naked back and the swell of her flanks. She took me in her hands and guided me into the hot slippery depths of her and my skin was suddenly on fire and my mouth dry and my heart pounding and when I came that first time, it was as if the constellations in the night sky had flared and filled my eyes with fire.

Her name was Elizabeth and I remember after that first time, when we made love in meadows of clover flecked with hearts ease and wild orchid, how she had shown me her body, taken me between her legs and pulled my face into her, pulling the lips of her pussy apart and directing my tongue onto her small, sweet, slippery clitoris. I remember sitting with her in the rackety beech woods at Appleshaw, and through the green swell of the trees, watching a solitary Spitfire bank and loop high above in the clear blue sky. Unable to leave each other alone, we had sat on the banks of a stream, feet on the rounded stones in the cold water, arms around each other. When I close my eyes, I can still summon up her breasts, little more than muscles on her skinny chest, the taut hollows at the top of her legs, her musky thighs, the coldness of her bottom marked from the dewy grass where we lay naked in the damp evening, and the heat of her soft, wet lips. We had made love noisily in dusty barns while the nightjars rasped outside in the corn and small animals blundered about in the rustling bales.

She would sometimes smile at my attempts to slip myself inside her and once when she kissed my poor, rock-hard, fragile erection and I came into her red mouth, I had nearly died. But she had laughed, and in The Hatchet, late at night while the moon hung above the hill like a flaming eyelash, she would come to my room and I would wake to find her sweet, silky mouth on mine.

~

Anyway, after driving for a while through the narrow Hampshire lanes, I came upon The Hatchet squatting like a thatched cake under the dying sun. It had lost the air of untidy rustic splendor I remembered and I knew as soon as I turned off the engine that there would be condom machines in the gents and the landlord would own an Alsatian. Some kids were sitting close together round a table on the lawn in front of the building, while others fooled about with a football in the carpark. When I say kids, I mean men and women who have just left school and are at the end of a weekend in the country where they have been to a party on Saturday night and spent Sunday squirting city-bred hormones about in the country air. As I put my hand on the latch, a boy with thick hair and a pink shirt called across to me, 'Excuse me sir, I don't think they open until seven.'

Mortified at being called 'Sir', I wandered into the extremities of the garden, sat on a bench in the shade and opened my copy of *The Night Manager*. Sunlight was filtering through the leaves of a copper beech and dappling the grass, while pigeons, roosting, occasionally mating, exploded out of the hedge behind me. My cock, forlorn and pale, lay dormant beneath the folds of my grey flannel Daks. I began to wonder why I had come.

At five past seven, there was the sound of a key being turned, latches drawn, a door being opened. A van pulled into the car park decanting two men in jeans smeared with plaster who started joshing with the barman and laughing at their own repartee, while outside, the kids, their intimacy destroyed, climbed into sports cars and drove away.

I ordered a pint of Otter bitter and some nuts for which a thin, humorless girl behind the bar charged me £2.70. The Hatchet had become one of those gnarled new country pubs; an inglenook, blackboards and Thai fishcakes on the menu. Round the corner in the bar, a hidden woman was talking furiously to a nodding man with grey hair and a submissive face. I wandered through a doorway and looked around for some sign which might rekindle a memory, but I was followed by the girl who said, 'That's our dining room,' in an accusing way as if I was planning to settle down at one of the regimented tables and drink my beer.

Sitting by a low window, my book open, my glass in my hand, I became aware after a while that the conversation in the bar had ceased. The barman and his companions had become silent and were looking at me, as was the woman, who had appeared, red-faced with tight, curly hair from behind a pillar and was giving me a hostile look. The barmaid was watching her, smiling faintly.

I tried to think of something to say, and glanced at my flies to check that they were secure. I looked out of the window and in the distance I could see someone on a bicycle, pedaling between shaggy hedgerows, pink with dog rose. There was something familiar about the figure, the cocky tilt of the shoulders, the long legs moving up and down beneath the billowing skirt. Attached to the handlebars was a wicker basket in which sat a small dog.

The red-faced woman coughed and I turned towards her. 'Excuse me,' she said, and I looked up into her face, at the tracery of veins about her nose, the clenched smokers' eyes. I presumed she was the landlady. 'Now then, what do you want here?' she asked. I looked out of the window again, at the figure on the bike whose distant face was beginning to harden into a strong chin, eyes wide apart.

She was tall, her head raised as if she was drinking in the country air and savouring it like wine. I looked again at the woman standing before me. 'I just want a drink,' I said, 'A pint of bitter and a bit of peace, if that's all right with you.' I was beginning to feel as if I had become trapped in a secret world, as if the pub existed in a universe of its own.

The woman continued to stare at me and I had the impression that she had been chosen as a spokesman. She commanded my attention. 'Well, why are you reading your book upside down?' she asked triumphantly, spitting out the words as if they were the closing sentence of a hostile cross examination. I examined the book, an old hard-backed first edition sent to me by David Cornwell in 1993. I had been putting off reading it. I could see that at some stage, I had removed the dust jacket and replaced it the wrong way round. It crossed my mind that perhaps they thought I was a spy.

I removed the book cover and slipped it on the right way up, took a mouthful of beer and stood up, winked at the barmaid and walked out into the dusty autumn evening. The woman on the bicycle had disappeared. I wish I could have watched her pedal past because, although I had seen her for no more than a few moments, I knew it was Elizabeth. As the light turned gold, I drove slowly out of the village, up the hill towards Chute Forest, through the arches of beech and oak until I reached the cross-roads and the signpost to Tangley.

I climbed out of the valley until, at last, I saw the bike leaning against the gate. It was a Raleigh ladies' bicycle of great antiquity, heavy, upright frame, large wheels and a metal chain guard. When I pulled up on to the verge I was certain she was nearby because I could scent a recent disturbance in the air, like the faint scent of perfume in an empty room.

I found her sitting at the top of a field, her back against an oak tree, her face tilted up towards the dying sun. The terrier had scampered down through the thick grass in a noisy attempt to see me off and Elizabeth had watched as I walked up the slope with the dog, friendly now, licking my hand and wagging its tail.

'Hello, Charlie,' she said, smiling. 'Long time no see.' I sat beside her and looked down across the field at the wooded valley below. Not a house in sight. From here it seemed as if nothing much had changed. 'I don't know why I came,' I said. 'I thought maybe you were still at the pub or something. It was just the spur of the moment.' 'I'm surprised you remembered me, Charlie,' she said. 'I left The Hatchet a long time ago and live on my own in the village.' I wanted to ask her if she had ever married, what she did for a living, but I felt guilty. I had never called her or even written to her after those delirious summer nights. I had simply gone home to London and resumed my life. The weekend had been like a dream and, riddled with the insecurities of youth, I was certain that she would have rebuffed me if I had tried to keep in touch. Eventually I had washed her from my mind.

'I went to The Hatchet,' I said, 'and I saw you cycling past. It's all Thai food and regulations now. They would never have closed on a hot afternoon in the old days.' She smiled dreamily and looked at me. 'Did you meet the owner?' she asked 'Mrs. Cleaver?' I described the furious looking woman with the red face.

'I didn't stay long,' I said, 'in fact I didn't bother to finish my beer. She was very unfriendly; perhaps she's got a drink problem.' Elizabeth glanced at me and smiled. 'Well, of course, you can never recapture the magic of your childhood,' she said, 'but I'm sorry you didn't like Mrs. Cleaver.'

'Why?' I asked her. 'The woman's dreadful. She's not just angry, she's rude.'

Elizabeth took my hand. It was the first time she had touched me since I kissed her goodbye all those years ago. 'When my father died,' she said, 'he left the pub to me and I ran it for 30 years or so, then my daughter married and I gave it to her and her new husband. They're divorced now, of course, gone their separate ways, but The Hatchet is still in the family. Mrs. Cleaver is my daughter, I'm afraid.' I squeezed her hand.

'I'm sorry,' I muttered. 'That was stupid of me, I should have realised, but I didn't recognise you in her at all.'

'Well, Charlie,' she said, glancing down at my hand, 'she's not just my daughter, I'm afraid. She's yours as well.'